SOUTHERN WANDS

SWEET TEA WITCH MYSTERIES BOOK TWELVE

AMY BOYLES

LADYBUGBOOKS LLC

ONE

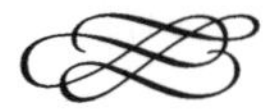

"Get in here. We've got some serious planning to do."

Rufus Mayes, my one-time nemesis and sort-of friend, had just informed me that the Head Witch Order was on its way to Magnolia Cove, Alabama, with the sole purpose of seeking me out for my power. They wanted to use my power for themselves.

That wasn't cool, y'all.

This meant we had to come up with a plan and fast.

Rufus crossed the threshold of Betty's house, and I slammed the door, closing out the night.

He stood inside and pinned his gaze on me.

I hadn't always trusted Rufus. In the past I would have preferred leading an alligator hunt in a swamp over believing a word he said.

But this time was different.

"What do we do? How can I stop them from doing anything to me?"

Rufus shook his head. "You're asking me to teach you how to gain the skill level of an advanced witch in the span of one night. Because that's what it will take to fight them off."

I nodded hopefully. "So you don't think it'll be a problem."

His expression twisted in frustration. "It's a huge problem. Pepper,

I can't teach you years of magic that quickly."

I cringed. "Are you sure? There must be a spell somewhere that will help me fake it. You know, fake it till you make it?"

Rufus scowled. "You're asking for the impossible."

"Aren't you a warlock? Surely you know something."

Footsteps hit the top of the stairs. "What's all this racket?" My grandmother's voice.

I groaned.

I debated hiding Rufus—shoving him in a closet and telling my grandmother a ridiculous lie that I was talking to myself. But what was the point? She'd know I was fibbing and would ferret Rufus out—probably by sniffing around the house.

Literally.

"Pepper? Is that you?"

"And Rufus," I answered.

Betty paused. I could tell she was deciding if she was going to be hopping-mad Betty or gracious-hostess Betty.

I sighed and closed my eyes tight. "The Head Witch Order is on their way."

Betty didn't bother taking the stairs. She appeared right in front of me in her bathrobe and slippers.

My grandmother glared at Rufus. "Are you their messenger?"

Rufus shook his head of dark hair. "No. I found out and came to warn Pepper. They're coming for her."

"Because of the issues with the werewolves?" Betty said.

Apparently there had been a dispute between some witches and a pack of werewolves. The Head Witch Order was now getting involved.

Rufus nodded slightly. "What started as an argument quickly became a skirmish—at least from what I understand."

Betty inspected Rufus from head to foot as if to make sure what he said was true.

I turned to Betty, hoping that maybe what Rufus predicted was wrong. "What will the Order do? And please don't say take my powers."

Betty pulled her glasses from her nose and cleaned them on her robe. "They'll take your powers."

"Crap." I raked my fingers through my hair. "I was hoping that was only worst-case scenario."

"That is if you don't offer to help them."

I shot Rufus a confused look. "You didn't tell me I had a choice."

He stared at the ceiling, silently asking God for patience, I was sure. "Ask Betty what they'll want you to do, and then you decide."

I glanced at Betty. "Well?"

She pulled her pipe from her robe. A flame flared on her fingertip, and Betty dipped it into the bowl, lighting the tobacco.

Way to stall, Grandma.

"They'll want you to do things...bad things." She slumped into her rocker and stared at the everlasting fire crackling in the hearth.

"Like what?"

Her gaze slashed to me. "Hunt werewolves. They may want you to kill them."

"They'll definitely want her to do that," Rufus said.

I winced. "I won't kill anybody. Axel's a werewolf. That would be like killing him."

"Only some of them will be women," Rufus said.

I shot him a dark look. "So you're saying it won't be like killing my boyfriend."

"Unless he has breasts, I would say not."

"Rufus," I yelled.

He shrugged. "I'm only telling you the truth. But talking about the nuances of biology doesn't help. What do we do with you?" He turned to Betty. "I can't teach her what she needs to know in one night."

"Maybe you won't have to," Betty mused.

I shook my head. "I don't understand why these witches think they can walk in and take whatever they want. Why are they so powerful? So feared?"

Rufus and Betty exchanged a look. "You can field this one," she said.

Rufus crossed his arms and leaned against the wall. A slash of dark hair fell over his eye, covering one side of his face. He pushed it away with a finely sculpted hand. Rufus looked so natural in Betty's home.

I wanted to hit myself over the head. There was definitely something wrong with me—like brain damage—if I thought Rufus Mayes looked perfect standing in my house.

"The Head Witch Order is an old sect of witches, dedicated to training only those with head witch powers, like yourself. They deem themselves as the elite. Only head witches are allowed membership, but the Order often finds itself tangled up in problems, like the werewolf issue."

His dark gaze bored a hole straight through me. There were times when I felt that Rufus could look into my soul and see the string that connected a part of me to him.

I guess that was why I never wanted to give up on Rufus. I knew a good soul lived inside him. Sometimes it was buried, but it existed.

"The Order will see you as theirs. When they come, you have to do what they say. There are no arguments. They take what they want without question and without hesitation."

I balked. "Because they *can*?"

"Yes," he said quickly. His hand twitched. I felt he wanted to reach out to me, but we both stood unmoving. "They'll want you to fight their war with your powers. You can either join their ranks or they'll take what they want—no exceptions."

Fear surged from my head to prick my toes. The hair on the back of my neck rose as a chill swept across my flesh. No wind rushed through the house. It could only be fear coursing through me.

"Betty, is there anything we can do?"

She tapped the stem of her pipe to her lips. Suddenly mischief flared in her eyes. "There is one thing."

Hope buoyed in me. She had a plan, and when Betty had a plan, it was either brilliant or horrible.

Let's hope this was on the side of brilliance. "What's that?"

Betty dragged her gaze from Rufus to me. After a long moment she said, "We hide you."

TWO

"It won't work."

Axel Reign stood in the middle of the living room, arms crossed, aggressive scowl slashed across his face.

To be fair, I didn't know if the scowl was because Rufus was in the room or if Axel just plain thought Betty's plan was stupid.

It could've gone either way.

I twisted my hair over one shoulder and knotted it at the end. "Why won't it work?"

His cool blue eyes settled on me. A chill zipped down my spine, encircling my heart. The power of his stare made my stomach quiver, my head swoon.

Powerful magic tangled up between us.

"Because," Axel said gruffly, "they'll smell the plan out. They know you're here. They'll find you."

"Not if we cloak her together," Rufus argued. He pointed to me. "If they come, Reign, the Order won't stop at just taking her. They'll make sure no one wants to play hero as well. They may take over the entire town."

I fisted my hands. "We won't let them."

"You won't have a choice," Rufus snapped. "They've done this sort of thing before—after another town sneaked behind their backs. The Order discovered it and took over everything. They outrank the local police, at least according to the High Witch Council. The Order can do whatever it wants."

"Then how can we hide Pepper?" Axel growled. He shot Betty and Rufus hard looks. "We're talking about powerful head witches." He raked his fingers through his ebony hair. Axel's biceps popped, and his straight jaw clenched in anger. "How will we keep Pepper safe from their magic? So that they don't discover we're hiding her?"

"We'll use magic they won't expect," Betty countered.

"What's that?" Axel said.

A slow smile curled on my grandmother's lips. "We'll use the dragon. Use his power to help."

Rufus dragged his gaze to Axel. The two men studied each other. Neither looked away.

I started to wonder if they were having an old-fashioned staring contest.

I almost clapped to break the hold.

"It might work," Rufus said.

"If it's done right. But if this goes wrong..." Axel warned.

Rufus opened his arms in invitation. "What? You'll take me out back and spank me? I'm trying to help. I discovered they're coming, and I want to stop it. They have no right to take her powers."

"Oh, now you see the light," Axel fumed.

Rufus smirked. He shook his head in disgust. "I saw it a long time ago."

Axel pointed his finger at Rufus. "We probably have you to thank for putting them on her scent. How do we know you didn't inform the Order about Pepper for revenge?"

Rufus's eyes narrowed to slits. "Do you really think I would do that?"

Axel took a threatening step forward. "I don't know the depths of what you're capable of."

Rufus stiffened. “I wouldn’t harm her—either intentionally or unintentionally. Can I say the same for you, *wolf?*”

You could practically hear Axel’s restraint snap in two. The insult of being called a wolf instead of a werewolf, as well as the reminder that in that past Axel had nearly attacked me, broke him.

He rushed Rufus, and in less time than it took for a raccoon to steal an apple from a trash can, Axel had Rufus pinned to the wall by his neck.

I moved to stop them, but Betty held me back. “Men must be men,” she whispered. “In order for them to feel like they’re protecting you, you must let them be. It is nature, nothing more, and you can’t hinder it.”

“You will take that back,” Axel growled.

Rufus stared at him, his eyes full of anger. “I won’t take anything back. Every word I said is true.”

“I could crush your windpipe.”

Rufus smirked in secret triumph. “I still have magic. I utter one command and you’ll turn into the wolf. Would the bond you share with Pepper be enough to rein you in? Would it hold? Or would you destroy those around you?”

I pulled away from Betty. “That’s enough. Rufus, shut it. Axel, stop! Let him go. He came to help.”

Slower than molasses dripping off a stick, Axel pulled away. But he glared at Rufus as if the man had eaten the last helping of banana pudding.

“I’m watching you,” Axel said in a low voice.

Rufus straightened. He had enough pride that he wasn’t about to rub his neck and show Axel he’d been bothered. But I knew Axel’s actions had cut into Rufus.

Rufus’s past would haunt him everywhere he went. No matter how much good he did.

He slid a hand over his hair and smirked. Rufus’s eyes glinted with danger. “Haven’t you told me that before? That you’re watching me.” He bowed slightly. “Watch me as much as you want. I’m only here to help Pepper and this town. To keep them safe.”

Feeling that their testosterone-fest was over, I turned to Betty. "How do we use Hugo to hide me?"

She slipped her pipe into her pocket. "Get the dragon and I'll show you."

THE THREE OF us stood in the living room. It was late. I didn't bother looking at the clock to know that. All I knew was that I'd be useless the next morning.

"Hugo," Betty said, "when I tell you to, I want you to breathe fire."

Hugo, my adolescent pet dragon, cocked his head in question.

"It'll be okay, boy." I smiled encouragingly. "You do as Betty says."

He pressed a cold, wet nose to the back of my hand. I ran my palm over the scales on his head. "What happens after that?"

Betty glanced at Rufus. He stepped forward, ignoring the flaming arrows shooting from Axel's eyes.

"You'll have to breathe in his fire," Rufus explained.

My knees wobbled. "I'm sorry. I think I heard wrong. It sounded like you were saying that Hugo was going to breathe deadly fire into my mouth."

"That's what he said," Axel replied.

"Oh, no sir." I backed away. "I know y'all want to keep me safe, but breathing fire is not the way to do that. I don't have a death wish."

Axel crossed over and placed his hands on my arms. His gaze drilled into me, making my breath hitch in the back of my throat.

Which then made me start coughing.

Axel patted my back until I got ahold of myself. "Sorry," I croaked.

"Let's try that again." Axel gripped my arms. His blue eyes pinned my heart to my spine. I wanted to fall into him, but now was the time to be strong.

"Hugo's fire is the most powerful thing in this room," he explained.

"Speak for yourself, wolf," Rufus said.

Axel ignored him. "The fire can mold with you and protect you.

This is stronger than any simple glamour. The Order won't be able to penetrate the dragon fire. It's the only way to hide you. If they appear and can't find you, the Order will leave."

I pressed my fingertips to my forehead. "I don't know."

"You have to trust me," Axel said.

"Us," Rufus added.

Axel shot him a look that could've burned his skin right off. "Stay out of this."

Rufus sighed dramatically and glanced away.

Axel hooked a finger beneath my chin and lifted it until our gazes locked. "Do you trust me?"

I nibbled my bottom lip. This wasn't about trust. It was about staying alive, and I didn't think literally breathing fire would do much to keep me that way.

But we were talking about magic and with magic, many things were possible. Not all, of course, but some.

"Yes, I trust you."

Axel's hand slid down my arm until it reached my hand. He threaded his fingers through mine and lifted my hand to his mouth, brushing his lips along the back of it.

My skin flared to life as his lips branded me.

His eyes never once left mine. "Are you ready?"

I swallowed a knot in the back of my throat that felt the size of Texarkana. I nodded.

Axel cocked his head to Rufus. "I'll need you over here."

Rufus's voice oozed with sarcasm. "Finally I'm needed. To what do I bestow this honor?"

"You're needed for Pepper; now stop your childish yapping and let's get to it," Betty said. "We'll need to make sure the spell works before the witches arrive."

I stood in front of Hugo as Betty chanted. Magic the size of lightning bugs flared and floated about the room.

Energy swirled around me. Axel took one of my hands, and Rufus took another.

I was acutely aware that Rufus's thumb was pressed into the wedge of skin between the thumb and forefinger. I could feel the calloused pad as he lightly stroked my flesh.

My gaze flickered to his.

Can you still hear me? he asked inside my head.

I hadn't heard Rufus for ages. The last time I remembered was when he'd worked a horrible spell on me that shifted my power to him—but only when I used my magic.

My throat dried at the idea that he could be in my brain. I had Axel. I didn't need to get my feelings confused.

I quickly glanced away without answering. Hurt filled Rufus's eyes but only for a moment.

"Ready, Pepper?" Betty said.

My head jerked in her direction. "I'm ready."

"Open your mouth."

Against all my better judgment, against all that was good and holy, I opened my mouth wide.

This was going to kill me, I just knew it. I would die by my own familiar's hand—or flame. Why everyone thought this would end well was beyond me.

"Now, Hugo!"

Betty lowered her arm as if signaling to two race car drivers that the Indianapolis 500 had started.

Hugo's mouth opened, and I stared at the soft flesh of his ribbed throat. From out of nowhere, fingers of orange and red shot from his mouth and slammed into me.

I thought it would hurt, I really did. I thought it would feel like I was literally on fire because, well, wasn't it supposed to?

But it didn't. At least not at first.

I felt nothing but air, and then the air turned cold. So cold I became frigid. At the point I thought I couldn't take any more, Hugo stopped.

"Hold her steady," Axel barked.

I felt myself fall. The cold was too much. Every cell in my body burned with fire from the chill. It was like I'd been blasted with a gigantic case of frostbite. Freezing pain raged all the way to my bones.

I drifted toward Axel, felt myself falling, toppling over. I couldn't see. Everything was white, and then suddenly it all faded away.

"Pepper," I heard Axel said. But he was so far away. I couldn't cross the distance. Finally he stopped calling and I slipped into a lake of ice.

THREE

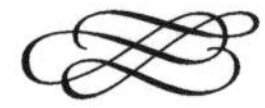

I didn't wake up until the next morning. My head weighed a ton and my movements were slow, as if I'd drank half a bottle of Benadryl the night before.

"Ugh," I groaned.

"She's waking." Rufus's voice.

I tried to blink. It felt like someone had jammed gum into my lashes. I had to work to pull them apart.

"Easy," Rufus said. I felt his hand on my arm. "The fire isn't something everyone can take. It has residual effects."

I exhaled a deep shot of air and forced my lids open. Rufus sat beside me on the couch. A cast-iron pot of greens and grits bubbled on the hearth.

Betty plopped a scoop of the thick, gummy concoction in a mug and handed it to Rufus.

"Eat that," she commanded. "It'll help you get over the chills."

"What chills?"

That's when the chills hit me so hard I doubled over. "A blanket! I need a blanket!"

Rufus took my shaking hands in both of his. "Pepper. Calm down. Eat this. It will help."

I nodded my trembling head. Rufus spooned a mess of white and green toward my mouth.

"I can do it," I argued.

"No." His eyes held a ferocity I wasn't used to. "You can't hold it. I'll do it."

So I sat while Rufus fed me. He was careful, making sure nothing dripped from the spoon. He also didn't overly fill the bowl. Every mouthful was perfect even if it was humiliating. But true to Betty's word, the chills disappeared after a couple of minutes.

"Where's Axel?"

"Doing intelligence." Rufus handed the cup to Betty. "He wanted to find out the location of the Order."

My gaze flickered to the floor.

"He wanted to stay," Rufus added.

"But he didn't trust you to find out for him," I said quickly.

Rufus's eyes hardened, but he said nothing.

"When are they supposed to arrive?" Cordelia entered from the kitchen.

"Soon." Rufus rose from his position by the couch.

I swiveled my legs to the floor. "Where's Amelia?"

"Work." Betty lidded the pot. "I told her to stay away for a little while."

"Why?" I said.

But no one answered because Axel swept into the house like a spring tornado, arms and legs moving at lightning speed.

"They're here." He propped his back against the shut door. His gaze cut to me. "How do you feel, Pepper?"

I nodded. "Fine."

"Can you stand?"

I shrugged. "Haven't tried."

Axel practically shoved Rufus out of the way as he lifted me to my feet. My toes gripped the floor, and my heels stayed steady.

"How's that?"

I wiggled my toes, making sure I stood solid before answering. "Better. I'm okay."

Axel gave me an encouraging smile. The corners of his eyes crinkled like a fan. "Stay strong. This will be an experience."

"Everyone get to the table," Betty commanded. "Rufus, you stoke the fire. Pretend you're working a spell. Axel, you help." A line of sweat sprinkled Betty's brow. "Pepper, you sit at the table; Cordelia, you set it. I'll bring the food."

I moved slowly, shuffling over on wobbly knees. Axel took my arm. "What's the plan?" I said.

"You're Amelia," Betty answered.

My eyes flared. "What?"

Axel explained as he escorted me to a seat. "She's a real person. She's not here. It's a perfect glamour that the Order shouldn't question."

"So I'm going to look like Amelia?" I gripped the arm of a chair and sank onto it.

"Yes." Betty gently rested the pot of greens and grits on the table. She pressed her hands to my shoulders. "This won't hurt a bit."

It felt like warm water was being poured over me. It drifted to my feet and was over as quickly as it started.

"Well done." Cordelia gave me an encouraging smile. "You look exactly like her. Make a few airheaded comments and it'll be perfect. Let me just text Amelia and remind her not to come here—"

A knock on the door made everything stop. Silence strangled the living room. I shot a fearful glance to Betty, who took a long look at me and nodded. She swallowed audibly and waddled to the front door.

Rufus and Axel took their positions by the fire. Rufus started mumbling something about a work-around spell, and Axel dragged his gaze from me and fixed it on the hearth.

The knock sounded again. I exchanged an uncomfortable look with Cordelia, who slid her phone onto her lap. She placed her hands on the pot and lifted the lid.

"Look normal," she whispered.

"I'm coming," Betty griped at the door.

I exhaled a deep shot of air. If anyone was a pro at looking relaxed, it was Betty.

She gripped the door handle and turned. I held my breath, unsure of what would stand on the other side.

The door seemed to shoot back on its own, as if a swift breeze had grabbed it and forced it open. Betty shuffled to one side.

Two witches and one wizard stood on the porch. The wizard, the tallest of the three, was positioned in back. He wore a long gray robe with a cowl pulled over his head. A beak-like nose peeked out, and dark, beady eyes stared blankly ahead.

In front of him stood two witches. The witch on the right wore a cape with dark feathers shooting from the shoulders. Her crystalline eyes glinted with intelligence or insanity, I couldn't tell which.

Nestled in her hand was a long, narrow wand covered in what appeared to be poison ivy. *Leaves of three, leave it be,* so the saying went.

The witch on the left wore a long golden robe. Her dark hair was pulled back softly from her face, and she wore long red gloves that came up to her elbows. She cradled a wand wrapped in silver.

"Can I help you?" Betty said as if three strange people appearing on her doorstep was an everyday occurrence.

Let's face it, this was Magnolia Cove. Strange things happened almost daily.

The crazy-looking witch on the right spoke. "I am Lacy Mock." Her voice was high-pitched and hard. Almost tinny. She pointed to the witch to her right. "This is Bee Sowell and the wizard is Hermit Mage."

Bee smiled warmly, and Hermit nodded.

Lacy hooked her gaze on Betty. "We are from the Head Witch Order."

"You don't say," Betty said. "Come on. All of you. I've just set breakfast on the table. There's plenty of grits and greens. If you can wait a few minutes, I'll fry up a mess of eggs and bake biscuits so fluffy you'd be hard-pressed to find any that taste better."

Lacy shook her head. "We're not here on a social visit."

Betty pulled out her pipe and tapped it against her palm, emptying it. "What sort of visit are you here for, then?"

Lacy took an intimidating step forward. "We're here for Pepper Dunn. We understand she's been living here."

Betty scratched her scalp with the stem of the pipe. "She was. Moved out a little while ago. Decided she wanted to live with regular folks. See, she never got to know her power and never really took to our ways."

"Who's been running the familiar store?" Lacy asked.

"Me," Betty said quickly. "I'm not as good at it, but until we find another person talented enough to take over, I'll have to do."

Lacy glanced over at Bee, who hiked one shoulder.

Lacy pointed at Betty. "I don't believe you."

"Search the house," Betty offered. "Search the town. You won't find her here."

Lacy's eyes twinkled with malice. "I will, starting with this room."

She fixed her prickly gaze to the left, narrowing in on Axel and Rufus. She stared hard. Axel's forehead broke into a sweat and Rufus tensed.

When she glanced away, they relaxed. I hadn't seen one iota of magic leave her body nor had I felt any magic drifting in the room, but Lacy must've used something to illicit that sort of response from the men.

Her gaze danced over Betty until it landed on me. I sucked in a deep breath and held it.

That was when the pain started. It felt like someone had taken a sledgehammer to my forehead. It was like this witch was trying to peel back my head one layer of skin at a time to get at the truth of me.

Intuition told me that all I had to do was stay strong. Take the pain; it would be over in a minute. But that minute seemed to stretch forever.

Finally Lacy's gaze flickered to Cordelia and I was off the hook. Cordelia glared arrows of fire at Lacy the whole time.

Lacy released Cordelia and turned to the other witches. "Search the house."

"You can't just walk in and search," Betty snapped.

"We can and we will." Lacy raised her poison ivy wand. "We have the right to do whatever we want. The High Witch Council listens to us. They will do what we ask."

Betty grumbled something under her breath but stepped out of the way. The witches swept into the house, disappearing in three different directions.

Lacy floated up the stairs. I exhaled a deep breath. My gaze met Axel's. He gave me an encouraging smile.

None of us spoke. The only sound was the ticking of a wall clock as it notated the passing seconds.

A few minutes later Lacy tromped down the steps. A second sound followed her. It wasn't until her toes touched the floor that I saw what it was—Hugo.

My heart rate ticked up a notch. Surely this meant nothing. I forced myself not to stare at Betty, not to make contact with Axel or Rufus, not to let the fear threatening to strangle me gain hold.

"Whose dragon is this?" Lacy asked.

We were silent.

She glanced down at the floor, her expression thick with impatience. When she thrust her gaze back on us, anger filled her eyes. "I will only ask one more time, who does this familiar belong to?"

"It was Pepper's," Betty said quickly. "Obviously she couldn't take it with her, so she left it here."

"In whose room?"

"It stays in Pepper's old room. Makes a mess in there. Likes to lay on her clothes, so I leave some out for him."

It was the best lie I'd ever heard as my room was never tidy. There was always at least one article of clothing on my bed.

Lacy's mouth curved into a suspicious smile. "Since no one here owns this dragon, he comes with me."

My heart lurched. I shot Axel a frantic look, but his gaze remained leveled at Lacy.

Bee and Hermit joined her by the door. "We will continue to look for Pepper. There's important work we need her for. In the meantime, if you hear anything from the woman, let me know."

Lacy flicked her wand, and a business card framed in flames flared to life. Betty plucked it from the air.

The witch twisted her wrist, and the door opened. Amelia stood directly in their line of sight. My cousin quickly took in the Order and then the rest of us, until her gaze settled on me.

I opened my mouth to say something, to stop Amelia from giving me away, but it was no use.

"Pepper," she gawked, "why do you look like me? What's going on?"

Lacy, Bee and Hermit turned back. Lacy's mouth curled into a snarl. "Well, well, well. It appears Pepper Dunn hasn't left Magnolia Cove after all." Lacy wagged a chastising finger at my grandmother. "Your attempt to hide her didn't work."

Lacy took an intimidating step toward me. "Rise, girl. You're coming with us."

FOUR

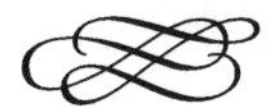

I rose. Lacy pointed a finger at me, and I felt the glamour wash away.

"I'm not going with you. I'm not going to fight werewolves, and I won't be used by an Order I know nothing about."

Lacy stiffened. "They're threatening our people. This is not about what *you* want. It's about the safety of all witches."

Axel stepped forward. "Werewolves don't wage war on witches. Not without cause."

Lacy glared at him. "Stay out of things you know nothing about. Wolves are encroaching on our land. Taking what they want by force. This is not a joke."

Bee stepped forward. "We're asking for your help." Her voice was like birdsong—light and comforting, as if her magic resided in her throat. It was a net cast out to catch all who heard it. "Please," she added.

Lacy shook her head in disgust. "We will only ask once. You are needed. Your powers will add to ours—whether you give them or we *take* them."

Rage bubbled inside me. How dare these witches waltz in and command me this way and that.

I closed my fists. "I won't go anywhere."

Lacy's mouth curled into a hateful smile. "You don't have a choice. You will come with us. You will help—one way or another."

Bee frowned. She flicked her silver-wrapped wand in the air. "But it's easier if you come with us."

"What? Than be taken and my powers drained from me? Is that what you mean?"

Bee yanked Lacy's dress. "Maybe we should let the woman make up her own mind."

"No," Lacy said. "We don't have enough witches to help us."

"Wonder why," I whispered under my breath. Lacy's eyes darted to me, and I took a big bite of courage. "It's no wonder, really, is it? You walk in demanding people do what you want, against their will."

"Enough!" Lacy bunched up her hands. She took a deep breath and slowly released her fists. "We have spoken to you nicely, and you have said no. Now you will come with us."

She took a threatening step forward. Axel and Rufus both moved to stop her, but Hugo beat them to it.

Lacy opened her hand while Hugo's jaw unhinged. A line of fire spewed from his mouth.

The witch raised her arm, shielding herself with magic. The fire shot to the ceiling, scorching the exposed wooden beams.

Hugo's wings flared. The immature wings he'd had as a baby were no more. In their place spread leathery, cobwebbed sails that were nearly ten feet long from end to end—if I had to guess, that was.

It wasn't like I had a measuring tape on me.

The blaze receded, and Lacy stared at us. Her gaze flickered back to Hugo, and she paused.

The witch sniffed the air as if a bad smell had wafted up her nostrils. "You can remain today, Pepper Dunn, as I see there are more of you than there are of us. But I will call in more of the Order. We will overrun this town to the point that the folks in Magnolia Cove would rather hand you over than keep you."

Her lips coiled into a cruel smile. "Mark my words."

Lacy threw her cape over one shoulder and, with a flick of her wand, vanished. Bee and Hermit followed suit, disappearing moments behind her.

Amelia stepped through the open door. "I'd ask what I missed, but I think I'm pretty much filled in on everything."

Axel's gaze dragged over each of us until it finally settled on me. "We've got a lot of work to do if we're going to be ready when they return."

Betty nodded. "First thing, Pepper—you've got to learn to use your magic. It'll be the only way to protect yourself. Otherwise they'll snatch you in the night and none of us will know where they've taken you."

I nodded slowly. "Who will teach me?"

Rufus stepped up. "I will. I know the most about your head witch powers. I'll do it."

Axel studied Rufus but said nothing about the offer. "I'll see what I can find out about this skirmish with the werewolves. Discover where it is and what's going on."

Betty ran her thumb down her jaw. "All they might need is an ambassador to straighten out the mess. You'd be the best person."

Axel nodded. "We've got a lot of work ahead. When Lacy returns, it'll be serious. She won't take no for an answer a second time."

My lower lip trembled. I bit down and waited until the tremor stopped. "How long do we have?"

All faces turned to Rufus. He shrugged. "Days, maybe. Hard to tell."

Betty rubbed her hands together. "Then let's get to work."

"THE FIRST THING you must do is learn to see your magic."

Rufus and I stood in the Cobweb Forest. He said it was the most honest place to work.

"This forest holds no opinions about you or your power. It won't judge like a person's house might."

I'd quirked a brow.

He'd smirked in amusement. "You don't believe me?"

"I wonder if you hit your head while you were gone from Magnolia Cove."

He'd chuckled. "No, not that time at least."

We'd both laughed, our gazes snagging until I looked away, playing with my hair to break the tension.

Rufus walked to an ancient oak as wide as a kitchen table and leaned against it. He wore leather pants, a leather duster and a black shirt. He plucked a twig from the ground and bent it until the wood bowed.

"You were saying I'm supposed to see my magic."

He nodded. "Close your eyes."

"How can I see if I close my eyes?"

"You might see better."

I stared at him in disbelief. Rufus moved his hand from his chest to his waist. "Close them."

I did as he said. Grass crunched beneath his feet as Rufus crossed to me.

"I want you to see the stick." He spoke beside my ear. The hair on the back of my neck rose.

One of the last times I'd seen Rufus was a few months ago, when he'd moved back into town. Things had been normal then—meaning we'd talked about life, regular stuff.

But now, while he whispered in my ear, I felt his raw power—it was like a box of electricity dying to be used. Rufus was a strong warlock, and to forget that would be deadly.

For anyone.

"See the stick," he repeated. "See it and take it."

"With my eyes closed?"

"Yes."

I knew where Rufus was, obviously, from the sound of his voice, and the most sensible thought was that the stick was still in his hand.

I felt my magic flare, and I directed it toward his hands, yanking at them.

"Nice try, but I don't have it."

"You tricked me."

"Never." He stood in front of me now. "Try again. This time, no tricks. See with your eyes closed, with your witch's eye."

I smirked. "What's a witch's eye?"

He sighed. "What all head witches have. It's what makes your powers so unique, why your gifts are limitless."

"How do I open it?"

"Here." Rufus touched his fingers to both my temples. An electric shock zipped down my skull to my back.

"Sorry," he murmured. "My power is flaring today."

Let's hope that's all that he had flaring. I shook my head, forcing the thought from my brain.

"Relax and I'll help you."

I exhaled a deep breath, acutely aware of his closeness. Body heat wafted off him onto my bare arms, electrifying the hairs. I could hear the faint beating of his heart, his inhalations, and even the rustle of his clothes as he shifted his body.

"Hold on," Rufus said.

My brain snapped to life. There was no other way to describe it. It was like someone had lit a torch inside the dark recesses of my mind.

"The stick," he reminded me.

As soon as he said the words, I could easily see it. Light flowed from my fingertips and zeroed in on the twig. I easily saw it as if my eyes were open.

"Put it in your hand, but keep your eyes closed."

I nodded. Rufus moved to the side, and I stepped easily, one foot in front of the other until I stood in front of it. Then I reached out and plucked the stick from the sky, where Rufus had suspended it.

The sound of him clapping filled my ears. "*Brava,* Pepper. Well done."

"Can I open my eyes?"

"Yes." I turned to see him beaming with pride. "You did it on your first try."

"You helped."

He shrugged. "I only unlocked what was already within you. You have the sight. But now how do you use it?"

I gestured in question. "How do I?"

"What did you see before you found the stick?"

"Light took me to it. It showed me."

He smiled. "That light is an extension of your magic. Now that it's open, you can use it for almost anything."

"Including defending myself?"

"That most of all." Rufus retreated one stride. "That's what we're going to do next."

My eyes widened. "We're going to fight?"

"Exactly. We'll start slowly, with your eyes closed."

I groaned.

"It's not that bad. Close them. Time is of the essence, Pepper."

I did as he said, curious as to how this would work.

Turned out I didn't remain curious for long. In the darkness, his hands flared as if they were on fire. I could see his power as easily as if I was looking at it in full daylight.

Rufus's arms moved back, and then magic shot from him. Instinctively I crossed my arms in protection. Ribbons of light wove into a shield that his power could not penetrate.

Good, he whispered inside my head. His voice was soft as a feather, lightly caressing my mind. *But it isn't enough to block; you must fight back.*

In the past, when I wanted someone gone, I'd projected as much on them, wanting them away. What usually happened was that they would fly back. But with the light extending from me, I knew I could do more.

I wanted Rufus bound, made unmovable.

Light flew from me, entwining his hands until the halo surrounding his fingers sputtered out.

"Well done. Open your eyes."

I opened them to see Rufus brush his hands, effectively untying the knots I had bound him up with.

"That was a good start." He opened his palm, and a water canteen appeared. He offered it to me, and I drank greedily. Cool liquid sloshed down my parched throat.

"How do you feel?"

I paused, considered the question. "Plum tuckered out."

He smiled. "You're tired. That's normal. Now that you're actually using the magic buried inside you, that's what you'll feel. You'll find it's easier to use up your reserves and become tired. It's normal. Don't fight it."

I exhaled. "Okay. What else?"

"Now let's spar with your eyes open. This time I won't be so easy to defeat."

Rufus assaulted me with what I could only describe as using a hundred hands to distract me. He tugged my hair. Pulled my pants legs, untied my sneakers. It was literally the most annoying attack I'd ever undergone.

But when I looked for him, I couldn't figure out where the magic was coming from. I did the only thing I could think of; I used the light to throw his spell back on him.

"Good," he shouted when he dispelled my attack. Rufus wagged a finger proudly at me. "You just threw my spell on me. That's incredibly hard to do, but you managed it. You naturally improvised spell creation."

I cocked a confused eyebrow. "What?"

He smirked. "You aren't bound by words or formal spell training, so you create your own. It works well because you aren't confined to the restraints of what you know spells and magic to be—for you power is limitless. As well it should be for any head witch."

I tried to wrap my brain around what he'd said, but I found it challenging.

"Now what?" I said.

"I will teach you Lacy's weakness."

I hiked a brow. "How do you know it?"

"Because I know her," he said coolly. "I know many witches and wizards, even warlocks."

A hint of jealousy stirred inside me. I shoved it back into the dark hole it had come from. "What's her weakness?"

"She uses fire magic. A lot. Your best bet will be to use ice against her—if it comes to that."

"Do you think it will?"

He picked up a stone instead of answering. "I want you to turn this into ice."

I stared at him as if he had lost his mind. "It's a rock."

"Turn it into ice. It's not hard. Changing it into something else is simply one part wishing, one part asking."

"Oh well, if it's that easy," I said sarcastically.

"It can be. If you let it."

He tossed the stone, and I plucked it from the air. I felt the cool weight of it. "One part wishing, one part asking."

I stared at the smooth brown surface and imagined it was a snowball. I asked and then coaxed, teasing my ribbons of light over it.

It seemed to cool down, but then heat flared. The stone sparked, and it launched into my chest, knocking me flat on my back.

FIVE

Rufus knelt beside me. "Are you all right?"

Fog filled my brain. It took a moment for me to remember what had happened. But then I realized I'd been playing with ice—literally.

"I'm fine." I started to sit up, but Rufus pressed his palms to my shoulders. "Wait. Give yourself a moment. When you ask and it backfires, the magic often takes more of you than you realize."

I crinkled my brow in confusion. "What?"

He sat on a patch of grass beside me. "When you ask something to shift and change, you want something, so the magic takes your strength. All of magic is give and take. You can't always take without giving something. That's why potions exist, because in some ways it isn't simply a recipe you're making, but an offering, a gift to get what you need in return."

"You make it sound so…philosophical."

Rufus chuckled. He plucked a blade of grass and smiled. "I suppose it is. More theory than actual physics. It is magic, after all."

"Yeah, but that magic didn't do what I asked," I said, sulking.

One corner of his mouth tipped into a smile. "You can't master everything in one day. What would be left to learn?"

I studied him—the dark eyes, the fair skin, the ebony hair—he was such an open book but at the same time, a real mystery to me. "What do you have left to master?"

He stared at the sky whimsically. "Oh, I don't know—necromancy, how to raise an army of the undead to take over the universe, how to hold the ocean in my hand. The usual."

I shoved him playfully. "I'm serious."

"Who's saying I'm not?" Our eyes locked. We stared at each other and Rufus's lips parted to say something but he thought better of it and shook his head. "Come on. Time to get you home. I think that's enough for now."

"Rufus?"

He let the blade of grass fall from his fingers. "Hmm?"

"What did I do wrong?"

"About what?"

It was as if his question asked the world of me—much more than the simple answer I sought.

"About the stone?"

"You may not have asked the right way. It takes some time, the asking and wishing. Perhaps your mind was elsewhere."

He rose and extended his hand. I tentatively placed my hand in his, and he lifted me to him easily.

As we walked back through the forest, I realized that perhaps I had been wishing for something else all along.

"THERE'S BEEN a skirmish in a beachside town," Axel informed us. "The werewolves are a biker bunch. Apparently some witches came in on their territory, unaware it was claimed, and started taking over. They innocently caused problems, and now neither side wants to back down."

I cringed. "Is there anything we can do?"

Axel's blue eyes darkened to the color of a turbulent sea. "I can ask around, find out who's in charge and see if it's possible to get both sides to sit down, talk it out."

Betty dropped a skillet full of fluffy biscuits on the kitchen table. It sat beside a heaping plateful of chicken fried chicken slathered in white gravy.

"Y'all eat," Betty said.

Cordelia, Amelia, Axel, Betty and I sat at the table. Rufus had gone out to look around, see if Lacy and her band of evil witches had returned.

Rufus had been gone for hours. I was getting worried.

"It's not safe for you to go anywhere alone." Under the table Axel squeezed my hand. "Nowhere. You must have someone with you at all times."

"They might try to steal you," Betty agreed.

"But aren't there plenty of other head witches out there? Those more powerful than me?"

Betty and Axel exchanged a look. Amelia spoke up. "You've never been trained. Your power is raw. That's why they want you." She shrugged. "Or your power. It doesn't matter to them."

"That's why I told you that you needed to learn how to wield your gift," Betty added. "Because of fools like that Order."

Axel gave me an encouraging smile. His lips curved devilishly. "It'll be fine. Don't worry. They won't get you."

The door flew open, and Rufus strode in.

"He can just walk in now?" Axel snapped to Betty.

Betty rolled her eyes. "I'll take all the help I can get."

"They're here," Rufus said. "Lacy's returned with reinforcements."

"Is it bad?" Betty said.

Rufus covered his mouth. When he his hand away, he spoke. "Come see for yourself."

We rushed from the table to the front door. It took a moment for me to realize, but standing on every corner was a witch or wizard in dark robes.

"It's like that throughout town," Rufus explained. "They're everywhere—keeping watch, intimidating citizens, you name it, they've got the lock on it."

Lacy's voice boomed through the clouds as if God had handed her a megaphone. "All we want is Pepper Dunn. Pepper, turn yourself in to the Head Witch Order and we'll leave. Remain here with your guards, and we will take over your town piece by piece until you don't recognize it anymore."

I frowned.

Lacy's voice continued. "From this moment forward, Magnolia Cove is on lockdown. No one goes in or out, which also means the food supply will be rationed. A member of the Order will dole out your weekly supplies."

Lacy's voice hardened. "When what's on hand is all gone, then I'm afraid it's either give up Pepper or starve."

SIX

I gritted my teeth. "I won't let this town suffer because of me."

"What about Garrick?" Cordelia said. "Maybe he can help."

Betty pulled a pouch of tobacco from her blouse pocket. Instead of filling her pipe, she opted to chew it outright. The stress must've cracked her. Things must look bad if Betty was chewing tobacco instead of smoking it.

I might as well go ahead and turn myself in to the Order.

Just kidding.

"Garrick can't help," my grandmother answered. "If the High Witch Council approved the Order's actions, he's bound to follow the rules. Plain and simple."

"I don't want to be part of any witches that allow this Order to come in and do whatever they want," I argued.

Axel rubbed my shoulders. "We can't go to the council. Some of the members are tight with the Order. They turn a blind eye to Lacy's antics. There's no way to know who to trust on the council."

"But Lacy isn't joking. She'll starve our town for me."

"There's food to last awhile," Rufus said. "Don't worry about it,

Pepper. No one's going to let the Order have you." His eyes darkened. "Not for their purposes."

As we watched out the front door, staring at the sentinels set into place, a bad feeling washed over me. I couldn't put an entire town in danger simply because I was being selfish.

Perhaps I could come to an agreement with Lacy. I twisted my fingers and ignored the knot in my stomach. The least I could do was try.

But how? I couldn't leave the house alone. Not that I wanted to see Lacy alone, but I had to do something.

As I stood watching the witch sentinels, other folks opened their doors. They looked outside as well, getting a good idea of what we were in store for.

As our neighbors took stock of the situation, I felt their gazes land on our house and inevitably me.

A shiver raced down my spine. Our neighbors might be my friends for a while, but once the going got tough, they'd turn on me.

I retreated from the doorway and excused myself to my bedroom. I had a plan to figure out.

Once I was there, I started to piece things together. I couldn't meet with Lacy, there was no way. But what about Bee? At least she had a kind look to her, enough to make me think she might not steal my powers and leave me for dead.

As I put my plan into place, a knock came from my door. I opened it and found Axel.

"They've called a town meeting."

I hiked a brow. "The Order?"

He nodded. "In one hour. Everyone must attend."

I nodded slowly. I felt my face crumple. Axel swiftly pulled me into his arms.

"It's going to be okay," he murmured into my hair. "Everything will be fine."

I curled my fingers into his shirt. "Axel..." Words caught in the back of my throat. This whole thing was a mess—all of it.

"It will be fine," he repeated. "Nothing's going to happen to you."

All I could do was shake my head. He pushed me back, and I stared at him. "Do you trust me?"

"Of course." Tears sprang to my eyes. Axel brushed them away with his finger.

"Then trust this. I won't let anyone take you." His blue eyes darkened. "Over my dead body."

"Don't say that," I snapped. "It could happen that way. With these people. With that Lacy."

He threaded his fingers through mine and pulled me toward the door. "At least I'd die happy," he joked. "Knowing I protected you."

I rolled my eyes. "I don't want that to happen at all."

He smiled playfully. "But it's a good option. You have to admit it."

As much as I tried to stop, a smile spread across my face. "Whatever. I'm not going to laugh about this."

He kissed the back of my hand. "Come on. Let's go see what these witches want."

Every person and animal left our house for the meeting, which was to be held in the park beside Bubbling Cauldron Road. There wasn't an enclosed space big enough to fit all the town, so outdoors would have to do.

Witches in dark robes still stood stationed on every corner. I shivered.

"These folks give me the creeps," Amelia mumbled.

I nodded. "You can say that again."

"I have a plan," Betty said.

Hope lifted me. "What is it?"

She snapped her fingers, and a round black circle filled her hand. My grandmother shaped it and placed it on her head.

I squinted at her. "Is that a beret?"

She nodded. "It is. How does it look?"

I shot Amelia a confused look. "I guess okay. I've never worn one."

"What's it for?" Amelia said.

Cordelia rolled her eyes. "She's starting a resistance movement."

My gaze washed from the black beret to my grandmother's shining face. "A resistance movement?" I repeated. "What?"

"We have to resist them, girls," Betty said. "We can't let these witches win."

"Okay," I said slowly, unsure of what any of it meant. "What are we supposed to do?"

"Help me resist," Betty said proudly. "We can't let them get the best of us. They can take our food, they can take our homes but they can't take our freedom."

"Okay, Braveheart." Cordelia patted Betty's shoulder. "You tell us how your French resistance goes. Let us know how we can help."

Betty's eyes glinted with mischief. "I'll be putting my first plan of action together soon. I'll let y'all know what it is."

"I can't wait," Amelia said gleefully. "This should be fun."

We arrived at the park. Folding chairs sprinkled the lawn. We found some and sat. Mattie the Cat and Hugo stayed beside us, waiting patiently for the rest of town to arrive.

Finally they did. Folks shuffled in looking confused. A few threw angry glances toward me. Garrick Young, the sheriff of Magnolia Cove, walked in looking so sour if I hadn't known any better, I would've thought he'd been sucking a lemon.

Cordelia motioned for him to come over.

"Craziest thing I've ever seen," he said. "Whole place is a mess. Got witches all over acting like they're the law."

"Can we do anything about it?" Cordelia said, her voice full of concern.

He nodded toward the darkly robed witches. "We're outnumbered, and I've been told not to move against them."

"Maybe our dads can wish us out of this situation," Amelia offered hopefully.

Betty shook her head. "That's too big a wish. You'd be asking your dads to get rid of a mess of witches. Even if they did, there'd be nothing to stop them from coming back."

"Wipe all their memories," she said cheerfully.

Betty shot her a sour look. "Too many."

"It was just a thought," Amelia whimpered.

"The resistance," Betty said in a dark, foreboding voice. "It's our only chance."

As more people spilled in, I glanced over and saw Bee walking toward the stage. Seeing that I couldn't slip away unnoticed, I tugged on Axel's shirt.

"I'm going to talk to Bee."

"I'll come with you."

"Alone," I demanded.

His jaw clenched. "You're not to go anywhere by yourself."

"She's different," I pointed out. "I know I can talk to her, reach her."

Bee had stopped and was talking to a wizard. He looked much younger than her. He had a curly head of blond hair and looked to be pleading with her. Bee shook her head. The look of anguish in his eyes made my heart lurch for him.

"No," Axel said.

Rufus spoke up. "Let Pepper trust her instincts. She *is* a head witch and may know better than most of us."

"Please." I searched Axel's eyes for a hint that he would relent. "I need to speak to her alone."

His mouth tightened, and he dragged his gaze from me, staring into the distance. "If you must."

I gave Rufus a small nod of thanks and took off toward Bee. When I reached her, she was alone.

"Bee," I said.

She pivoted her head over her shoulder toward me. It was as if in that moment she registered who I was. She whirled around, her silvery wand flashing in her hand.

"You shouldn't be here," she hissed.

Gone was the cool demeanor of the woman from yesterday. Bee appeared frazzled. She gripped my shoulders and pushed me between two magnolia trees.

She glanced around frantically. "What are you doing?"

"I wanted to speak to you. You seem like someone I can reason with. Unlike Lacy."

Bee's gaze darted left and right. "She can't be reasoned with. She'll do anything to possess your power. Girl, you don't know how much danger you are in."

"Yes, I do."

"She'll kill you for it," Bee admitted. Her gaze crumpled in misery. "I'm sorry to tell you that, but she will."

"Can't you talk her out of it?"

Bee threw back her head in laughter. "No one can talk Lacy out of a thing once it's stuck in her head. She's relentless."

"What can I do?"

Bee cringed, exasperated. "What can you do? Give yourself up unless you want your town to suffer." She wagged a finger. "Or worse, they'll turn you over." She closed her eyes as if a painful memory had bloomed inside her head. "Like they did me."

I curled my fingers into her robes. "You have to help me. Help my town. We must fight."

Bee shook her head.

"Bee," I begged. "Once you were like me. Once you were your own person, had your own dreams until I'm guessing they were stolen from you. Lacy has no right to do this. She wants me for some skirmish."

Bee shook her head. "That's only a front. The situation with the werewolves is coming to a head, but she wants your power simply because you don't know what to do with it—that's what all her reports said."

"What if we could calm the situation with the werewolves?"

Bee frowned. "Then she wouldn't have a leg to stand on—at least not officially. It would help." Bee pulled away. "I must go. We cannot be seen together."

"Won't you help me?"

Lines wrinkled her forehead. She smoothed them as if trying to iron away stored memories. "I shouldn't do it, but meet me tonight. Here. I'll think on how I can help. But," she said sharply, "I can't make any promises."

"Thank you," I said hurriedly.

"Go," she commanded.

Without hesitating, I went, racing back to my seat.

"I was about to come after you," Axel growled.

I snaked my hand through the crook of his arm. "Good thing I got back when I did, huh?"

He mumbled something I couldn't understand, and we turned our attention to the front of the park where Lacy now stood, flanked by Bee and Hermit.

Lacy raised her hands. "Good citizens of Magnolia Cove. The Head Witch Order has arrived in your town because our friends are dealing with an uprising with rogue werewolves."

Axel cursed at her mention of his kind.

"The Order specializes in using head witches for our purposes, but we are short bodies, my friends, and in dire need of extra help. We have appealed to your animal talker, Pepper Dunn, but she has refused to assist our kind."

Heat flushed my face. Murmurs washed through the crowd. I could feel the town's ire toward me. I hated it. I wanted to disappear. Go somewhere far, far away.

"We have appealed to Pepper," Lacy continued. "Begged her for help, but she has refused and set her pet dragon to attack me."

I closed my eyes. "Lies."

"And so now you have to suffer," she said. "If you haven't heard, your town is on lockdown. No one goes in or out. No food will arrive, either. Until Pepper Dunn turns herself in to the Order, all of you will suffer."

I cringed.

"Unless Pepper gives herself over right now, our occupation will move forward."

Lacy's gaze locked on mine. The entire crowd shifted, and I felt a thousand stares on me.

Her lips parted into a sadistic smile. "What do you say, Pepper? Would you like to give yourself up?"

SEVEN

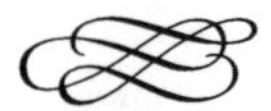

"No," Betty answered before I could. "My granddaughter ain't giving herself up to some lady who's trying to intimidate us."

Lacy smirked. She turned her gaze on Garrick Young. "Sheriff, arrest Betty Craple for dissension."

Garrick's eyes widened.

Lacy glared at him. "If you won't, one of my witches will do it for you."

Garrick crossed to Betty. "I'll handle you better than they will. Come on."

Betty glared at him. "You would arrest me?"

He cocked his head toward the robed witches and wizards. Most of them had a lust for pain in their eyes. "Would you rather they do it?"

"Good point."

Garrick escorted my grandmother through the crowd.

Anger pulsed in me. Lacy was a bully, pure and simple. In that moment I decided I would do whatever it took to bring her down.

"Would anyone else like to argue with me?" she asked the crowd.

I was shocked that no one answered.

Not.

She smiled viciously. "Good. We have an understanding then. Starting tonight you will be put on strict curfew. Everyone must be in their homes by nine o'clock. Anyone seen outside after then will be arrested—or worse."

I swallowed a knot in the back of my throat. Lacy might lock down this town, but no matter what, I would be out and about looking for Bee—whether Lacy caught me or not.

LACY SPOKE for a few more minutes. When it was over, we packed up to leave.

"Where's Hugo?" I said.

Axel shook his head. "He must've wandered off."

"We need to find him." I rubbed my arms, trying to slough off the bad feeling that was creeping in. Lacy hadn't liked Hugo. What if she placed a spell on him or sent someone to snatch him away when we weren't looking?

I felt Rufus's gaze on me. "He'll be okay," he said as if he sensed what I was thinking. "We'll find him."

I nodded sadly. "I hope so."

"Come on," Axel said. "Let's get you home before the curfew starts."

"Okay."

We headed back. My house was a verifiable fortress with Axel, Rufus, Cordelia and Amelia all sleeping in it.

As soon as we arrived, Cordelia set off to call Garrick to see about Betty. "I want to make sure she's okay."

I stayed downstairs with Axel and Rufus for a while before retreating to my own bedroom.

Mattie the Cat reached the bedroom before me and sprawled out on the bed. She blinked lazily at me when I entered.

"Don't you be worryin' 'bout that dragon, sugar," she said. "He'll be jus' fine."

"I hope so."

I stared at my shoes.

"What else is botherin' you?"

I sat on the bed. The mattress sagged beneath my weight, creaking and moaning in its familiar way. I curled one leg under the other and turned to Mattie.

"I need to get out of here tonight to meet Bee. She said she'd try to help."

Mattie yawned. "Let me guess—you want me to sneak you out of the house even though the entire town is on curfew and there's a crazy witch out there wanting to snatch you up."

I grimaced. "When you put it that way, it sounds pretty insane. But yes, that's what I need."

Mattie rose, arching her back and stretching her front legs. "It's against my better judgment, but I'm gonna do it. I'll help you. But you have to be quiet as a field mouse."

I smiled wickedly. "I will be."

"You gonna take Axel?"

"This is my fight. I wouldn't put anyone in danger. Besides, Axel wouldn't let me go by myself. He'd say it was too dangerous."

"He's right," she said.

I ignored that bit of judgment. "If I get caught being out after curfew, then I'd deal with the consequences alone—no matter how awful they were."

Thoughts of Lacy filled my brain. I shoved them aside and looked deep inside myself for my courage, which was usually not in short supply.

When darkness fell and it came time, I found my way back to my bedroom and locked the door behind me.

Mattie listened to make sure no one was heading up the stairs as I opened the window and stepped onto the roof. I shimmied down a drainpipe and landed softly on the grass.

Mattie appeared in the window. "Be careful," she whispered.

I nodded and ran off, sticking to the shadows. I reached the park alongside Bubbling Cauldron a few minutes later. I'd only noticed one witch out on patrol, and had easily evaded her by pressing myself against the side of a house until she passed.

I had at least one advantage—I knew my town. Knew all the nooks and crannies.

I arrived between the two magnolias that Bee had dragged me to earlier that day. I didn't know what time she would arrive, but I would wait all night if I had to.

As long as nobody figured out I'd left the house and no one caught me, I would be fine.

After a few minutes I noticed a dark shadow striding toward me. They were walking funny, stilted, as if their knees were locked.

Bee didn't walk like that, but as the figure approached, I saw her eyes glinting in the moonlight.

"Bee?" I whispered.

But something was wrong. Her face was charcoal black; so was the rest of her.

I rushed up. "Bee? What happened?"

She fell into my arms. I struggled to keep her upright but somehow managed.

Her mouth opened and shut, and her skin smelled burned as if she'd been roasted. Bile surged up the back of my throat.

Her clothes lay in tattered ashes. "Bee? Who did this? What happened?"

She worked her mouth, but no sound came out. Then her eyes shut. I laid her on the ground and felt for a pulse.

There was none.

Something bound up behind her.

I rose and tightened every muscle in my body. This was it. I would fight to the death if I had to. Someone had burned Bee to death, and I was ready for a fight.

The thing launched itself forward and landed at my feet.

"Hugo?"

My eyes widened with fright. Hugo craned his neck, and I extended my hand for him to sniff.

"Hugo, did you scorch Bee?"

A light snapped on in front of me. Lacy, Hermit and her gang of witches glared at me.

"Stop right there, Pepper Dunn," Lacy said coldly. "I've got you now."

EIGHT

"You've done it, Pepper," Lacy sneered. "You've killed one of us—a head witch in the Order." She smirked. "One of the three, in fact. You're in deep now. And look"—she pointed to Bee's hand—"it appears you've stolen her wand as well. It's missing."

"I didn't steal it."

Lacy approached me, her eyes glittering with happiness. I swear, I wouldn't have been surprised if her skin turned green and she started cackling about getting me and my little dog Toto, too.

Yes, she was that evil.

"I didn't do it," I said. "I didn't kill that witch."

Lacy scowled. "I know you did. I know you sent that dragon to kill her same as you tried to do to me!"

I shook my head emphatically. "I didn't. I swear. She was helping me."

Lacy gasped. "Bee was helping you? How dare you lie about that." She curled her hand around my arm and yanked me toward her. "We'll see about getting you help now. You have no choice but to do what I want."

Lacy dragged me away from Bee. Hugo rose into the sky and cut us off.

Lacy's hand swept over her body. "Do you think one of your kind is going to stop all of us? We outnumber you, dragon. Your mistress may have gotten you to kill my friend, but you can't kill the rest of us."

Hugo opened his mouth. I cringed, expecting fire to stream out, but instead he screeched. It was a sound full of anger and pain.

Lacy simply laughed.

"Get out of my way, dragon."

"Not so fast there."

A new voice made Lacy stop. She whirled around to see Garrick Young and a posse of his men circling Bee's body.

She eyed Garrick as if he was an unexpected guest who'd just declared he was staying for a month. "What do you want, Sheriff?"

A light flared in Garrick's palm. He knelt and inspected Bee's body. "I'd say this here is a case of murder."

"You think?" Lacy snapped. "I found Pepper Dunn standing over the body. Her dragon was here as well. The witch coaxed her dragon to kill a member of the Head Witch Order. She is a criminal."

He nodded. "Yep, that's what it looks like." Before Lacy could utter one word, Garrick marched up, took me by the wrists and slapped magical handcuffs on me.

"Pepper Dunn, you're under arrest for the murder of Bee"—he turned to Lacy—"what was her last name?"

"Sowell," Lacy answered.

His gaze shifted back to me. "Pepper, you're under arrest for the murder of Bee Sowell. You will come with me, where you will stay in jail until you are tried for your crime."

Lacy's jaw dropped. "What? You can't do that. You can't take my witch. She's mine. You know that."

Garrick shrugged innocently. "Lacy, with all due respect, you may've shown up in my town demanding this and that and outmanning me in some things. But when it comes to murder, investigating is still my job. Until Pepper is declared innocent, she's mine."

Lacy huffed.

Garrick's eyes hardened. "Do we understand one another?"

She nodded slowly. "We do."

"Good." He tipped his head toward her. "Now y'all have a good night."

Before Lacy could say anything, Garrick turned me away from the crowd. I whistled for Hugo, and he flew to us, circling the sky.

Garrick's men formed a wall around me, making me feel like I was surrounded by a human shield.

When we were far enough away that Lacy couldn't hear, I said, "Thanks for doing that. I appreciate it. Are you going to let me go when we reach the jail?"

Garrick shook his head. "Nope. You're going to jail all right."

It felt like a stone was plummeting down my stomach, falling fast to the very bottom of its depths. "What?"

Garrick glanced at me, annoyed. "I'm taking you to jail, Pepper. It's the only way to keep you safe."

"I was going to be safe," I argued. "Bee was meeting me to help me figure out a way out of this."

"And look what happened to her," he growled. "She's dead. Burned to a crisp. Didn't exactly turn out the way you planned, did it?"

"No, but—"

"No buts," he interrupted. "You could've gotten yourself killed going out after curfew. Or worse, taken by Lacy, and no one would know where to find you. What you did was stupid, inconsiderate. Now I've got a dead body on my hands, a town overrun with the Head Witch Order, not to mention a crazy woman running that show, and a murder. I've only got a shot-in-the-dark guess at a motive, so locking you up right about now sounds like the best idea yet. You'll be one less worry off my already heaping-full plate."

We'd reached the jail. Garrick escorted me in. Betty's eyes sparkled when she saw me. She sat in her cell, running a tin cup across the bars.

"Did they arrest you for being part of the resistance?" Betty asked.

"No. Murder."

Garrick opened a cell, and I walked inside, sitting on the cot.

Garrick pointed at a corner and a love-seat-sized doggie bed appeared.

"That's for you, Hugo."

The dragon obeyed him, curling up on the soft-looking bed.

"Who'd you kill?" Betty asked.

"No one," I snapped.

"Come on, boys," Garrick said. "We've gotta get back out and investigate the crime scene." He glanced at us. "I'm locking y'all in for the night. I'll tell Axel where you are, Pepper."

"Thank you."

He didn't reply, only left with his men. I heard the lock snap shut. It was the only goodbye I got from Garrick, and I found it a fitting exit for him.

"But to answer your question more completely"—I nodded to Hugo—"it looks like Hugo may have killed Bee Sowell."

"Not Lacy?" Betty said, sounding disappointed.

I bit back a laugh. "Unfortunately not, and if Garrick hadn't arrived when he did, that witch would've carried me off with her."

Betty clicked her tongue. "Good thing you're in here with me, then." She rubbed her hands together. "We can plan the resistance together."

I rolled my eyes. "How is that going to help anything?"

Betty pulled out her pipe, lit it with a tendril of magic that uncoiled from her nose, and sat back, puffing away. "I reckon the only way to get rid of these witches is to either get them on our side or run them out of town."

"How are we going to run them out of town when we're stuck in jail? It's not as if I can grab a pitchfork and start a witch hunt, for lack of a better idea."

"I've been doing some research," Betty said.

"On what?"

She winked at me, and a magical screen flared to life, hovering in the air. Lacy Mock's picture smiled eerily at us.

I shivered.

"This here is some information about Lacy. It talks about her interests—being head of the High Witch Council, destroying werewolves, possibly becoming part vampire—"

"Part vampire?"

"She has a lot of goals. Most of them sound like the ramblings of a crazy woman."

"Which is just great, seeing how she's head of the Order."

"She's only head for now," Betty informed me. "Next up is Hermit."

I clutched the cell bars that separated us. "When is her term up?"

"Lacy's term lasts five years. She's on the end of it now. Every few years the leadership shifts, and whenever there's a new one, everyone follows them. All who belong to the Order now follow Lacy, but put Hermit in charge—"

"And things will be different." I gritted my teeth. "But that's not for months. We don't have that long—days maybe before food starts running out. What are we supposed to do?"

"Our only other option is to flood the town with guinea pigs."

I rubbed my lips together as I tried to figure out if my grandmother had indeed said what I thought she had said.

"Did you say we have to flood the town with guinea pigs?"

"Lacy Mock is deathly afraid of them. At least according to this source."

I scratched my head. "You're suggesting that if we release enough rodents into Magnolia Cove, that will run her off?"

"If you had guinea pigs running up your skirts, you'd be hollering to get out too, don't you think?"

She had a point. If it was a true phobia, it could work. "But what about feeding them?"

"You've got a pet shop. You can feed them."

"I'm locked up in jail. A murder suspect."

She dismissed my concern with a wave. "Ah. We'll figure something out, but first things first—I think this is our best bet."

I had heard crazier ideas. Heck, I'm pretty sure I had *proposed* crazier ideas. But the more I thought about it, the more I realized we had nothing to lose.

I gave Betty a nod. "Go for it. Release the guinea pigs."

~

Nothing happened immediately. Since it was late, I decided the best thing to do was get some sleep. When I awoke the next morning, the first person I saw was Axel glowering at me.

I wiped crust from my eyes. "You look mad."

"I'm livid."

I clicked my tongue and said jokingly, "Ooo, I'd hate to be the person on the receiving end of your anger."

"*You* are that person."

I winced. "Oh. Right. I guess you're mad that I left the house."

His jaw clenched. Fire practically shot from his eyes. "You were supposed to stay at the house. How hard is it to understand that you're in danger? How difficult *is* that? Then I discover when you leave, you walk right into Lacy and it's a miracle that she didn't snatch you up."

"There was a dead body," I offered.

"And it looks like Hugo did it at your bidding. I'm aware of that. I also know that if it wasn't for Garrick, you wouldn't be here."

I smiled brightly. "But I am."

"I'm still mad."

I rose and reached through the bars. Axel backed away. "This is serious."

I threw up my hands. "What did you want me to do? Bee told me she could help, so I met her. I didn't want to put anyone else in danger."

"Instead you put yourself in danger," he shouted. "And you could've gotten killed. Or worse, stripped of your powers, leaving an empty shell of who you once were. Do you even know the danger you're dealing with?"

I stared from Axel to Betty. I was missing something. They were keeping things from me, and I was ticked. "No, I don't, because no one tells me anything!"

Axel's eyes narrowed.

Betty said quietly, "She's got us there."

Axel shot her a scathing look. He took a few steps back and pointed to Rufus. "Tell her what happens. Then maybe she'll understand why we're trying to protect her."

"Why won't you tell me?" I said weakly.

His nostrils flared. "Because I'm so angry I can't talk to you right now. I'm afraid of what I'll say."

His words were an arrow to my heart. It felt like a lightning bolt had cracked my ribs apart and sliced my heart in two. Never had I made Axel so angry that he didn't want to speak to me.

At least, I don't think I had.

Rufus approached slowly. He gave Axel a searching look before starting.

"Lacy Mock once got ahold of a young woman named Claire who had the potential to become an exceptional head witch but lacked training, same as you. That wasn't Claire's fault. She tried to learn, but there were few masters who could teach her what she wanted to know.

"Under the guise of the Order, Lacy found Claire and promised to help her rein in her power and unleash it in ways Claire could never imagine."

Rufus smiled bitterly. "Of course Claire accepted this. Why wouldn't she? The opportunity to excel as a head witch was more than anyone had ever offered her before."

"So she didn't know anything about Lacy?"

"No one did. Not at that time. So the two women met, and whatever happened between them—well, I won't go into the details, partly because I wasn't there and partly because much of what I think is speculation. But anyway, when all was said and done, Lacy delivered Claire to a home for witches who'd gone insane. But Claire wasn't insane, she was simply a shell of her former self, someone who couldn't hold a fork to eat or a pencil to write."

My jaw dropped. "She became catatonic?"

"To put it mildly," Axel said.

I grabbed the cell bars and pulled, knowing it would do no good, but I had to do something with all the anger burning inside me. "Why didn't any of y'all tell me this?"

"Isn't it enough to know she's dangerous?" Axel snapped.

"No. Keeping me in the dark is like treating me as if I'm a child. I'm not a child. I'm a grown woman with a business. I deserved to know that about Lacy."

Rufus gave Axel a hard look. "I didn't know all of it for certain until a couple of days ago. We thought it best not to say anything." He lifted his palms and hiked his shoulders in a shrug. "After all, what good would it have done you to know this? How does it help anyone?"

"Would you still have gone to meet Bee if you'd known?" Axel said.

My gaze darted to the floor. "Probably."

He shook his head with disgust. "This isn't a game."

"I'm not asking you to take up for me," I snapped and immediately regretted it.

The hurt in his eyes shredded me, crushed me, destroyed me so completely.

"I'm sorry," I said.

He took a step forward until his chest brushed the bars. He whispered so that no one could hear but me. "I want you safe. I'm sorry if that's so hard for you to accept. Men protect women. It's a part of life."

"I deserved to know that."

"And now you do," he said. "You're welcome."

I had no words. When I glanced into his blue eyes, I knew the only reason we fought was because my ego was getting in the way.

I opened my mouth to apologize when a scream split the air.

Betty chuckled. All of us turned toward her.

She winked at us. "That would be the guinea pigs. I do believe they've arrived."

NINE

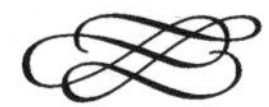

Outside was pure chaos as I watched through the windows of the jail. Brown guinea pigs, black guinea pigs, even orange guinea pigs scampered through the streets.

There were so many it was like a tidal wave of rodents had burst into Magnolia Cove.

Betty cackled like the witch she was. "Look at that—sheer perfection."

I watched a black-robed witch kick a guinea pig from her leg. "What about our own citizens?"

Betty nodded to Rufus, who smiled sheepishly. "Someone got a message to them that they should remain inside for a few hours this morning. Not go out."

I gaped at him. "That was really nice of you. Thank you."

"Here comes Lacy," Betty said gleefully. "I knew she'd want to see the prisoner first thing this morning. Ha! She got caught right in the middle of a stampede."

Lacy Mock stood like stone in front of the wave encroaching on her. Her eyes ballooned to saucers as she realized exactly what she was facing down—a city of rodents.

She grabbed her skirt and ran straight for the jail.

"Great," I murmured. "Why couldn't she have run in the opposite direction?"

"Too easy," Betty said.

Unfortunately for Lacy, a branch of guinea pigs moved to cut her off. Before she reached the door, they swarmed her, covering her body, even her face.

The jail door opened. Dang. I guess Garrick had unlocked it for Axel and Rufus. I should've told one of them to lock it back.

Lacy shrieked. Tears streamed down her face as the guinea pigs rampaged over her legs. She kicked and they scrambled away.

"Get off me!" She clawed her arms, and half a dozen rodents scattered to the floor. One cute little guy, caramel and white, ran right through my bars and under my cot.

Lacy managed to get the last of the creatures off. She glared at them as they scattered across the floor, disappearing under furniture and out of sight.

She heaved a deep breath before lifting her gaze and turning it to us.

Her voice trembled. "How did they get here? Who did this?"

We shook our heads. Betty shrugged. "I don't know. Must've been a herd of 'em outside town before you arrived. That happens sometimes—herds of guinea pigs storm through. You just got to weather it."

"That's right," I said. "It's not my first rodeo with that lot. They're ornery little critters—like to stay for ages before moving on."

Lacy's head trembled with anger. "You called them here. I know you did. Get rid of them or I'll destroy this entire town. I won't wait to starve y'all out!"

Betty's eyes hardened to flints of steel. "You do that and my friend over there will turn into a werewolf and rip you to shreds."

Lacy's gaze flickered to Axel. "He can't become a werewolf whenever he wants. That's impossible. Werewolves turn at the full moon. No other time."

Axel took a threatening step toward her. "Want to try me?"

It was a bluff, a very good one, but Lacy didn't know that.

Her gaze drifted around the room, landing on each of us before she turned her attention to Betty. "It seems we're at an impasse." She circled the jail, her footfalls hitting the floor heavily, in a dramatic fashion. "You won't let Pepper go, and I want her. And now I have even more reason to want her because she killed my friend and stole her wand."

Friend? Likely story. From the way Bee spoke, there hadn't been any friendship there.

"I didn't kill Bee, and I didn't steal her wand. This town is in the middle of a murder investigation," I said. "I can't leave."

Betty thumbed toward me. "She's the prime suspect."

"But I didn't do it," I snapped. "I didn't kill Bee. I had no reason to."

"Didn't you?" Lacy said, eyes glittering. "Maybe you thought she was me. Maybe you figured if you got rid of us one by one, we'd leave you alone."

There was one thing I knew, that I wasn't the killer. Yet I couldn't stay locked up in this cell for weeks while Lacy starved my town.

There was one option that would help me, though—or kill me. Not sure which but it was my best option.

"I challenge you," I said, "to a duel of magic."

Lacy's jaw dropped. She eyed me suspiciously. "You do what?"

"I want to challenge you to a duel. If I win, you leave me and my town alone. If you win, you can take me with you."

"No, Pepper," Axel said.

"But I need time to prepare," I added quickly. "We can't do it today. While I'm getting ready, I want you to promise that I can walk around freely. I won't be harmed, and the people here will have access to food. You won't starve them."

Lacy threaded her fingers and brought them to her chin. "It's an intriguing offer you've made, especially for an untrained witch such as yourself."

I shrugged. "What can I say? I believe in my abilities."

"I believe there's cotton between your ears," Betty grumbled.

I ignored her. "What do you say, Lacy?"

"Wait, Pepper," Axel interrupted. He glanced at Lacy. "Before you answer, let me speak to her."

Lacy cackled. "Going to try to talk some sense into her?" She flicked her hand. "By all means, do so."

Lacy stepped to a corner, keeping an eye out for guinea pigs along the way.

"What are you doing?" Axel growled.

"So I guess this means you're even more angry at me?"

His jaw flexed in response.

"Look, you and I both know I didn't kill Bee. But what if it was —" I nodded to Lacy. "We need time, Axel. If we can prove the corruption of the Order, or even better, show that the conflict we've heard so much about isn't as bad as the hype, then we stand a chance of getting rid of them. But to do that we've got to buy some time. I need to get out of this cell. We need to find the real killer."

He gripped the bars. "But by challenging her? You're talented, but she's trained—highly trained."

"I'll study hard. Please," I pleaded, "it's our only chance."

He shook his head. "I'm not sure about that."

"Trust me." I didn't know why I said that because I wasn't sure what there was to trust. Axel was right. He hadn't said it, but I knew he thought my decision was reckless, that it was stupid to challenge Lacy. But the way I saw it, there was no other option.

Axel bowed his head and backed away from the cell. My gaze darted to the witch. "So, like I was asking, what do you say? Care to join me in a magical duel?"

Lacy's mouth coiled into a smile that made her lips look like they would stretch all the way to the corners of her eyes.

"I would be honored to join you in a duel. It will occur within one week. That gives you time to study, to see if you have what it takes to defeat me. But I doubt you do." She smiled wickedly. "You might as well start saying goodbye to your friends now. Oh, and I will still stop supplies from entering. I'll keep the curfew as well."

I swallowed a knot in my throat. I wouldn't let Lacy's intimidation techniques get the best of me.

I glanced at her feet. "Is that a guinea pig by your toe?"

Lacy shrieked and tossed her hands in the air. When she looked down, there was nothing there.

She glowered at me. I shrugged innocently. "Sorry. My mistake."

Lacy pinned her ire on Betty. "Get rid of the guinea pigs. All of them. Now."

Betty cracked her knuckles. "Not that I'm the witch who called them here, but let me see what I can do."

Betty chanted under her breath. I peered out the window, watching as the storm of rodents receded. They turned mid-run and headed out of town, back in the direction they had come from.

Betty smiled. "There you go. Safe travels."

Lacy grabbed her skirts and headed toward the door. She whirled around, fixing a glare on me. "One week. That is all."

The door opened by itself, and Lacy strode through, not looking once over her shoulder at us.

I deflated onto my cot. "Glad she's gone."

Axel stared at me. "What you've stepped into is worse."

I smiled weakly at him. "Oh, I don't know. It was between keeping the people of this town safe and my own preservation. I think I chose the wiser."

"We have a lot of work to do," Rufus said.

"I know. We need to get started today."

Betty huffed. "You can count on one thing for certain."

"What's that?" I said.

"Lacy won't fight fair. Not a witch like her. She'll do whatever she can to win, and that means she'll fight dirty."

I shot Axel a worried look.

He shook his head. "One reason I tried to talk you out of it."

"What do you propose we do?" I said.

Betty clapped her hands. The guinea pig that had hidden under my cot shuffled out and into her arms.

"How come that little guy didn't go with the others?"

Betty smiled at me. "I asked him to stay. I figured we'd need all the help we can get against Lacy."

"What's he going to do?"

She grinned wickedly. "This little guy is going to be the eyes and ears of the resistance."

"Pardon?"

"He's going to spy for her," Rufus said.

I pointed at the guinea pig. "That rodent is going to spy on Lacy?"

Betty nodded. "Most certainly he will." She scratched under his chin. "He'll tell us everything we need to know."

Okay, great. Now that I knew Betty was officially ready for the looney bin, I could at least think the rest of this situation was normal—like the insanity of me dueling against a highly trained witch, for instance.

"Just you watch," Betty added. "This little guy will give us serious intel."

"I'm going to talk to the werewolves," Axel said. "See what I can find out about the skirmish."

I stared at him. He studied me for a moment before glancing at the wall. "You're...you're leaving?" The words barely came out. They exhaled in a whisper that was barely audible.

"You have Betty and Rufus to keep you safe."

What? Axel didn't like Rufus. I wouldn't say he hated him, but he certainly didn't one hundred percent trust the man.

"When will you leave?"

"As soon as I see you safely home."

It felt like a hand had grabbed my heart and squeezed. My rib cage constricted, and my head floated like I couldn't get enough oxygen.

"I won't be gone long," he said soothingly.

I nodded, unsure of what else to say. Betty had the resistance, Rufus would train me and Axel would...leave. It was a strange chain of events.

"I'll be back within a couple of days," Axel said. "Long before you duel against Lacy."

That at least made me feel better. I pushed a smile to my face to show that I was strong. That all of this was okay and that we would come out on top.

Betty rubbed the guinea pig to her nose. "Okay, little guy, are you ready to go spy on Lacy?"

"You bet," he answered in a high-pitched voice.

Betty lowered him. "Then scat, find out everything you can and report back to me."

The rodent scurried across the floor, squeezing out the door through a small gap at the bottom.

Betty rubbed her hands together. "All right, Pepper. It's time to get you out of here."

The cell door vanished. I glared at her in surprise. "You mean you could do that the whole time?"

She shrugged. "I'm an old witch. I can do a lot of things." Betty nodded to Axel. "Say your goodbyes. We've got work to do."

I scrunched up my face, forcing away tears. Axel took my hand and led me from the jail.

We only had a few moments. Time to say everything to him I'd always felt but never admitted—at least not to him.

TEN

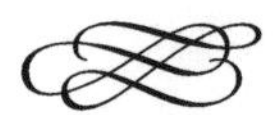

We walked slowly back toward the house. A few straggler guinea pigs ran this way and that, but otherwise the rodents had evacuated the village.

A humorous image of Betty playing a pipe leading the guineas from Magnolia Cove popped into my head. She was dancing and dressed like the Piped Piper.

I mean, she basically was, after all.

"I shouldn't be gone long," Axel repeated.

We walked through the park beside Bubbling Cauldron. I'd slipped my hand into his. His hand offered little comfort when what I wanted to do was throw myself onto him and beg him not to leave.

"I don't want to go," he said as if reading my mind, "but you're in good hands, and I can't exactly send Rufus to meet with the werewolves and become their best friend overnight."

I smiled widely. "Are you sure?" I teased. "I'm pretty certain Rufus could make friends with them easily enough."

He barked a laugh. "Not with his reputation."

"Shucks," I replied.

We were silent. The heaviness of the situation creeped in. I tried to dispel it, but it was no use.

"The other day—" I started.

"When I asked you—" he said at the same time I did.

We stopped. Stared at each other. I giggled nervously. Axel's mouth ticked up into a delicious smile. "Go ahead," he said.

I screwed my courage to my spine. "The other day, when you said..."

"Marry me?" he finished for me.

My gaze darted right and left. "Yes." Sheesh. I hated having serious conversations like this—you know, the kind where the *feels* were all tangled up.

"That's the conversation I'm talking about. When you said that..."

"I meant every word." He studied me sharply. His eyes narrowed, and his pulse quickened in his throat. "There were only two words, after all," he joked. "But I meant them both."

"Being with you is all I want." I took his hands in mine. "I know this is where our relationship is headed. I guess I've always known, but I've been scared."

"You think?"

I shook my head. "This world is full of so many unhappy endings. I just want ours to be happy."

He slipped his hand from mine and stroked my chin. "That's all I've ever wanted. I promise to do everything in my power to make it that way. I won't add to any more of your tears, Pepper."

I smiled. "One thing I wanted to know about myself was if I could make it alone. We took things slowly, not rushing in, and I needed to be sure I could stand on my own two feet."

"You can," he said proudly. "I've watched you do it."

"But there are other things I've had to deal with. I'm afraid of losing you. I've been afraid you'll get tired of me, bored with us." I cocked my head. "I don't exactly have a stellar track record with men."

He smiled. The edges of his eyes crinkled. "I'm different. I'm not all men."

"But you are *all* man," I joked.

He chuckled.

"I know I've pushed away from you. I know I haven't been easy to deal with, but I've been wrestling with my own demons. Trying to lay them to rest so that when we move forward, there's nothing standing in our way."

Axel grabbed my hand and tugged me to him. His lips claimed mine, and he drank from me until he had his fill and my knees quaked.

"There's nothing standing in my way of being happy," he said huskily.

I had to snatch at the words floating around in my brain to make them stay. I felt scattered to the wind, broken apart by him and free.

"I know what I want," I said. "I'm ready to answer your question."

He pressed a finger to my lips. "Wait."

I blinked. "What?"

"Until I return. Tell me then." He pressed my hand to his heart and smiled. "It'll give me something to look forward to, and make my trip faster if I know what I'm waiting for."

I narrowed my eyes. "Are you kidding?"

He shook his head. "No."

I scoffed. "You're going to make me wait until you return to tell you?"

He laughed softly. "You made me wait before you were ready to broach the subject, so I think it's fair."

I opened my mouth, shut it again. He was right. *Crap*. Axel was absolutely justified.

Oh well, I supposed I deserved it after I'd spazzed out on him when he first mentioned the words in his cellar while he was naked.

That was another story for another time.

I tipped my head back and let him kiss me again. "I guess I deserve that."

Axel grinned. "Come on. Let's get you to the house."

Before we could take another step, Rufus magically appeared in front of us.

"Sorry to disturb the two of you, but we have a problem."

Axel's shoulders tensed. "What sort of problem?"

Rufus nodded to the edge of the park, where a line of witches from the Order were marching toward us.

Panic fluttered in my throat. "What are they doing? Lacy called a truce."

"I guess they didn't receive the message," Axel growled.

"What do we do?" I said.

"Rufus," Axel said, "can you change me?"

Rufus eyed Axel apprehensively. "Now? On the spot?"

"Yes."

"Perhaps. But I can't guarantee the stability of the spell."

"Meaning?" I asked.

Rufus's gaze flickered to me. "Meaning it's possible that he'll remain a werewolf for a lot longer than intended."

"I'll have control," Axel argued. "I'll be present. Can you do it?"

The line of approaching witches neared. Rufus clenched his fists. "I can try."

Axel nodded with the resignation of a soldier being shipped off to war. "Do it."

Rufus started to chant and wave his arms.

"Axel," I said weakly.

His gaze snapped to me, and before I could speak another word, he said, "I love you."

Those were Axel's last words before fur sprouted from his flesh, his muscles grew, tendons split and his clothes ripped away as they became shredded rags.

Axel's face stretched. Fangs took the place of his human teeth, and dark whiskers erupted on his cheeks.

I sprang back, and the line of head witches stopped. Rufus took position beside me as the last of Axel's human self disappeared and he became the beast.

Axel? I flung my thoughts out at him.

The werewolf whirled around. He stared at me with yellow eyes. The tension between us was taut. It was like I stood on one side of a chalk line and Axel on the other. He would either hear me and respond, or because Rufus had forced the change, Axel wouldn't know me. Which meant I'd be at risk of attack, but so would the witches approaching us.

I'm here, he finally said inside my head.

I exhaled and nodded at Rufus. "He's with us."

Rufus strode toward the line of witches. "We are in a truce with you at this time. Lacy has given us her word. If you refuse to listen, you will be at the mercy of the werewolf."

Rufus smirked. "That's only something I would wish on my greatest enemy." He opened his arms in invitation. "All of you are welcome to try for the position of winner against him. At this time it's open."

The witches stared at us, and then finally a man spoke. "We will only listen to Lacy."

Rufus flashed me a grin. "I think I'm going to enjoy this." His gaze flickered to Axel. "They're all yours, wolf."

Axel's muscles twitched in anticipation. He bounded forward, leaping one story into the air.

The witches threw magic at him, but Axel's skin was tough. He threw himself into their midst, and the witches scattered like ants discovered stealing from a picnic.

The diversion worked. The witches were so busy warding off Axel that none of them paid attention to us. Tears spilled from my eyes as I watched him.

Rufus placed a gentle hand on my shoulder. "He'll be fine. He has enough of himself inside there to know what to do."

"But how will he escape the lockdown?"

Rufus smirked. "I believe your grandmother worked something out with the sheriff. Made sure there was a way to get one werewolf out of this place."

Hope bubbled in my chest. "But if it could work for him—"

Rufus shook his head sadly. "He's the only one of his kind in here. The shields would bend for him but not the rest of us."

It was probably a good thing.

Axel tossed a few of the witches in the air. They landed hard on their backs. The Order would be ticked about this.

"I warned them," Rufus mused. "I told them we were in a truce, but they didn't listen."

"Do you think they'll retaliate?"

He scanned the horizon. Axel stood panting as the last remaining witch ran in the opposite direction, away from him.

Rufus smiled. "No, I don't think they'll retaliate. I think they'll be too afraid to touch one hair on your head."

The wolf turned and stared at us. Then, without warning, he leaped into a copse of trees, disappearing from sight.

ELEVEN

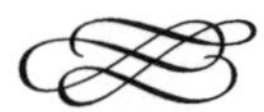

Axel's absence wasn't like a hole in my heart; it was more like a hole in my entire body. Even though Rufus and Betty told me not to worry, it was difficult not to.

"He'll let us know when he's arrived," Betty said. "Your Axel is a big wolf, able to take care of himself. He will find out everything he can."

"Do y'all even know where he went?"

Rufus dragged his gaze to Betty. "He asked us not to say. Just in case it got out."

Hurt sliced through me. "I deserve to know."

"He didn't want you to know for your own protection," Betty said. "Be patient, Pepper. He'll return."

"Better to be safe and sound," I mumbled.

"Let's focus on what we can," Betty said. "Cordelia, Amelia and I are working on the resistance. The guinea pig is in place discovering information. And you"—she turned her gaze to me—"must prepare for a fight with Lacy."

I nibbled my bottom lip. "Lacy killed Bee; I just know it. I only have to prove it."

Rufus snickered. "What are you going to do? Go up and ask her to confess."

"I had considered it."

He shook his head. "No. Your best bet is to discover how to fight her and win. I will help with that."

I wanted to argue, but I had put myself in this position. "Fine. Let's get to work."

"Good, because I have a new tutor for you."

I hiked a brow. "Oh? Who?"

One side of Rufus's mouth curved into a smile. "Just wait and see."

"WHERE ARE WE GOING?"

Rufus had transported us by magic to a hillside. I didn't recognize my surroundings even though the appearance of magnolias along with poplars easily meant we were on the other side of town.

"We're near the Conjuring Caverns."

"Oh," I said quietly. "Why'd you bring us here?"

"Because this is where you're meeting your tutor," he said impatiently. "Did you really think Lacy would allow you to practice out in the open?"

"I hadn't thought about it," I muttered.

"Well I did, and seeing as how I'm in charge of your education so you don't get yourself killed"—he shot me a sidelong glance—"then in the dark depths you will learn. It's best for all involved."

"Thank you," I said, humbled.

Rufus stopped. Stared at me. His jaw clenched. "You're welcome. Now. When you meet your tutor, don't scream. Don't be scared."

We had nearly reached the cave. Light splashed inside the open mouth.

"Why would I be scared?"

A dark figure stepped into view. He was tall with a cowl draped over his head. He held a lantern in one hand.

I stopped. A jolt of fear snaked up my spine. Rufus placed a calm hand on me.

He spoke through clenched teeth. "I said, don't be afraid."

"How can I not be afraid?"

"Because he's here to help you."

"Isn't that Hermit?" I locked my knees, stopping Rufus from pushing me forward. "But he's one of the Head Witch Order."

"He's also a friend."

I twisted my head to look up at Rufus. "Whose friend? Yours?"

"And yours. You have to trust me."

"I trust you. But he's one of *them,*" I whispered fiercely.

"Come now." Rufus pushed me forward. "You wouldn't want our guest to think you're not grateful for his help."

I stared at Rufus darkly. My knees unlocked, and he forced me along.

"Trust me," he whispered in my ear. "Hermit will help us. He'll help *you,* but you have to trust him."

I relented. "Fine. But I'm cautious."

Rufus's eyes widened in mock surprise. "You? Cautious? I'd love to see it."

Rufus led the way inside. Hermit stepped back, keeping to the shadows.

They clasped hands like old friends. "Hermit, thank you for coming. I believe you know Pepper."

He nodded slowly. Up close I saw the man's features. His face was thin, and his jowls sagged from age. His eyes were watery, but they held friendship, not the contempt I had figured most of the Order had.

"Pleasure to meet you, dear," Hermit said in a deep voice. "You are very brave to take on Lacy."

"Or stupid," I said.

He chuckled. "No, I don't think so. There aren't many of us who dare think differently than our leader. When we do, it tends to get us murdered. And to think she was once my protégé."

Lacy his protégé? Seemed Hermit had suffered a lack of judgment somewhere down the line.

I peered into his eyes. "Are you saying Bee was murdered because she went against Lacy's wishes?"

Rufus cleared his throat. "Perhaps it's best if we stick to your lessons, Pepper. Save the political talk for later."

Hermit nodded in agreement.

Great. I'm outnumbered.

But I did as I was asked, listening to Hermit. "I believe Rufus has told you of Lacy's propensity toward fire."

"He has."

Hermit extended his hand inside the caverns. "We will use this place to give you a glimpse of what fighting her might be like."

The last time I had been in the Conjuring Caverns was ages ago. The caverns had shown me my greatest fear, and it had been terrifying.

I wasn't sure I wanted to relive that element of terror, but if I wanted to survive Lacy, what other choice did I have?

"Grab a stone, young lady," Hermit commanded.

I did, palming the cool rock in my hand.

With his finger, Hermit drew a straight line in the air. Lacy appeared in front of me.

I gasped and rocked back, losing my balance and falling. Strong arms grabbed me before I hit the ground.

"It's only an image," Rufus murmured in my ear.

"It's dadgum good." I snorted.

Hermit spoke. "You will fight this image until you win. I cannot know exactly what Lacy will do, but I have knowledge and experience guiding me. You will fight fire with ice, yes?"

I nodded.

"Then go."

Lacy raised her arm. A spear of flames appeared in her hand. She bowed her arm back and flung the weapon at me.

I didn't have time to think. I begged the rock to become ice and flung it at the image.

The spear hit me in the chest. The flames disappeared, while the rock landed dully behind the smirking Lacy.

It hadn't even tried to transform into ice.

"You are dead," Hermit said.

"Can someone insert another quarter and I'll get my life back?" I joked, referring to video games.

Rufus tsked.

"I guess not." Sighing, I turned to stare at Hermit. He placed the lantern on the cavern floor.

"You must ask differently," he instructed.

"How? I don't understand how I can ask something that isn't alive to do something for me."

"That is part of the problem."

"What is?"

"You don't see the rock as living."

"It isn't."

"Are you sure about that?"

I stared at the unmoving stone. "Yes, I'm pretty sure."

Hermit slowly smiled as if he took great pleasure in feeling every inch of his face transform. "Until you learn to see, to really see, you will be limiting yourself."

I scoffed. "I saw some ribbons of light the other day. I can close my eyes and see magic."

Hermit paced the cave. "That is a good first step. Now you must see more, believe more."

"You want me to believe that this rock will listen to me?"

He nodded slightly.

Every cell in my body wanted to argue this. It made no sense. How was I supposed to ask an inanimate object to turn into something?

I decided to go with the phrase, *fake it until you make it.* Seemed like a good enough mantra for me at the moment.

I inhaled deeply and shut my eyes. "I will try."

"That is all we ask," Hermit said. "Try again."

I could do this. I knew it was possible. I only had to see inside myself, believe that I was capable of more than I was giving myself credit for.

Lacy's image raised the fire spear. I cupped the rock, asking, begging for it to turn into ice. The stone felt warm in my hand. A bubble of power popped from my palm, and I stared at the rock hopefully as Lacy unleashed the spear and it hit my heart.

"You're dead," Hermit said flatly. "Again."

"I was so close last time. Let me try," I pleaded.

"Until you conquer it," he said.

So I tried again.

And again.

And again.

Each time the magic bubbled in my hand, but that was it. Every encounter, Lacy killed me.

I worked with Hermit until it felt like someone had scooped all the magic from my body.

"I'm spent," I said after being killed by Lacy for the fiftieth time.

Hermit patted a rock beside him. "Come sit."

Rufus drifted to the front of the cave. "I'll keep an eye out here."

When we were alone, Hermit asked, "What is it you want most in life?"

I balked. Wow. I didn't know. I wasn't exactly one of those ten-year-plan people, but maybe I should start. Hmmm. Something to consider.

"I don't know…to be happy, I guess."

He nodded. "What is happiness to you?"

"It's being safe, secure. Knowing whatever happens, I'll be okay."

Hermit sat silently for a moment. "And how do you feel right now?"

"Right now I don't feel okay." Before I could stop myself, I blabbed everything to Hermit. "I feel like it was partly my fault that Bee was killed. She was coming to talk to me, Mr. Hermit. She was going to tell me a way that I could get out of this. I feel like no one cares that she's dead. The sheriff can try to find her murderer, but Lacy has made it clear that she's in charge. I don't know if he'll be able to ask the right questions—and what if Lacy was the person who killed Bee in the first place?"

I slapped my thigh in frustration. "What am I supposed to do about all this? Where's my happiness? I don't have any because my stomach is knotted up with worry."

He patted my knee. "My dear, until you put this anxiety to rest, you will never be able to do what you need to match Lacy."

"Oh," I said flatly. Crap. I felt like Hermit had just pulled the wind right out of my sails.

He inhaled deeply and wrapped his hands around his knee. "Bee may have been a quiet, kind woman, but that doesn't mean she didn't have enemies—even without your presence, I mean."

Wow. Was Hermit going to help me? "Okay. Who were her enemies?"

"With Bee gone as one of the three heads of the Order, another witch will have to take her place."

"Okay," I said.

"There will be a meeting tonight to discuss it. If you want to know who killed her, I would start there."

Hermit rose. I followed suit. "Where will the meeting take place?"

"At our camp. Where we are staying, near the Hangman Tree inside the Cobweb Forest." Hermit peered down at me, his silvery eyes flashing a warning. "You must quench this worry in your heart and this indecision."

Rufus entered the cave.

"I'm not indecisive about finding the killer. It's what I want."

Hermit turned toward Rufus. "That's not the indecision I was talking about. Tell me, son. Is it safe for me to exit?"

Rufus nodded. "The way is clear."

Hermit exited the cave without another word.

Rufus slowly crossed to me. "Well? What did he say?"

I cringed. "He said we have to infiltrate the Order's camp tonight if we want to find Bee's killer."

Rufus smiled wickedly. "Do we wear furs or silk, do you think?"

I stifled a laugh. "I would suggest we wear black."

As I walked out with Rufus, I wondered what Hermit was talking about, but even as my head was unsure, my heart knew one hundred percent.

TWELVE

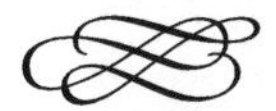

"Do you think you should put some sort of invisibility spell on us?"

Rufus and I sat in a thicket of wild hydrangeas. The leaves had all turned green and the smallest of buds were beginning to form on the branches.

Rufus stared through the bush to the gathering assembly. "I don't want to risk one of the witches sensing the magic. If they find us, I'm not sure the truce you have with Lacy would hold."

I shivered. Not from the cold but from the thought of what Lacy would do to me if we were discovered.

"Then I suppose we should be quiet," I said.

Rufus frowned. "I'm not the one talking."

I rolled my eyes. "Tomato, *tomahto.*"

He dragged his gaze back to the witches and wizards. "It didn't go well today."

"I'm still learning."

"You must learn faster."

"I'm trying," I snapped. "It's all I can do to focus on everything going on. Axel is gone, and I'm to be burned at the stake. It's kinda hard to concentrate."

"Burning at the stake," he said pointedly, "would probably be easier than enduring Lacy."

"Thanks for the vote of confidence."

Rufus scowled. "I have a world of confidence in you. Do you not see that?"

I regretted my words. "I know you do. I'm sorry. It's just..."

"What?" he said quietly. "You can tell me."

"It's nothing."

Silence blanketed us. I opened my mouth to speak, but no words came out.

"Say it," he said, not looking at me. "Whatever it is, say it."

Here went nothing. "How can you be around me?"

Rufus didn't hide the surprise on his face. "You would ask me that," he whispered.

"Axel asked me to marry him."

Rufus's jaw clenched. "And so he should. The two of you are meant to be together."

The pain on his face made my heart tighten. "I didn't say that to hurt you."

"Then why bring it up?"

"Because..."

He turned and stared at me.

"Why did you come back? Really?" I said.

He didn't skip a beat. "Why did you call me?"

"Because the way we parted was wrong. You've come so far. I knew you couldn't be bad. Not with me," I whispered.

He scratched a spot on his cheek. "What is it you want to hear? You want me to divulge my deepest secrets to a woman who can't accept those words?"

I fought back tears. "I know what is right and I know what is meant to be, but what I don't know is...why?"

He took my shoulders in his hands. "On this planet, on this entire earth, you are one of the few people that can hurt me. I came to you because I care. We have limits, Pepper Dunn. Those limits are set by you and by me—for what I was. Maybe I just feel bad about everything I've ever put you through. I'm only trying to make up for an evil past."

I shook my head. "That isn't true. You know it."

His mouth parted to say something, but stopped.

"I don't have any strength," I whispered.

Rufus leaned away. He cursed and shook his head. "You are under stress. Great stress. We shouldn't even be here."

An eruption from under the Hangman's Tree grabbed our attention.

Lacy stepped forward. "Unfortunately, because of an evil witch and her dragon familiar, we are short one of the three. Bee Sowell was a wonderful witch and served the Order well, but now we must find her replacement. I look to you, brothers and sisters, to find the person best fit to take her place."

Bonfires burned throughout the witches' encampment while large, elaborately designed tents dotted the open field on either side of the tree.

Lacy's eyes glittered in the firelight. "Now. Who volunteers to take Bee's place?"

The young man that I had seen Bee argue with the day of the commencement stepped out from the crowd of witches.

"I volunteer," he said.

He had a curly mop of blond hair and a round, cherubic face. "Who is that?" I whispered to Rufus.

Rufus leaned closer to me. "Sherman Oaks."

"What do you know about him?"

"Other than he's young? Not much."

"I watched him argue with Bee."

Rufus quirked a brow. "That is interesting. We might have to discover more about him. I'll see what I can find out."

A woman with long black hair strode forward. "I volunteer."

"Who's that?"

Rufus clicked his tongue. "That is Slug Worley."

"Slug?"

Rufus nodded. "She used to be one of the three before she was kicked out."

"What happened?"

"Apparently Slug was trying to recruit non-head witches into the Order."

Slug took her place beside Sherman. "And I take it that's a bad thing?"

"Most definitely," Rufus replied. "She's seen as pretty liberal on that front."

A short, fat man stepped forward. Rufus chuckled.

"What's so funny?"

"That," he said into my ear, "is Widdon Franks. Not only does he have a glass eye, but he's as mean and nasty as Lacy, hates anyone who isn't a witch or wizard and once tried to make himself lord of all witches."

"What?"

Rufus nodded. "He had his own coven of about two hundred beneath him. They lived in New Orleans, and from there he ran a thievery ring the likes of which that city had never seen."

"New Orleans hadn't seen a racket that bad?" I couldn't believe it. "Is that even possible?"

"It was until the High Witch Council discovered what he was up to and made him disband his followers. Widdon was pretty irked about it, from what I heard. But here he is, trying to climb the social ladder once more."

Widdon's belly shook at every step as he made his way over to Sherman and Slug.

"So now he wants a position as one of the three," I mused. "Seems like a good way for such a man to get his power back. But the only thing that bothers me about suspects other than Lacy is that Lacy didn't like Hugo and the fact that someone burned Bee makes it a quick jump to point the finger at my dragon."

"Lacy could have told any of them what happened," Rufus said.

"That's true, and now we have three witches ready to take her place." I tapped a finger against the bush. "How are we going to get time with any of them?"

Rufus smiled wickedly, and a shiver snaked down my spine. "Leave that to me."

~

WE SNEAKED AWAY from the Hangman's Tree and headed back to the house. I was just thinking about Axel when my phone buzzed in my pocket.

I slid it out and glanced down.

I've arrived safely. Out of wolf form.

"I would hope so," I murmured. "I didn't know wolves could text."

"What's that?" Rufus said.

I dismissed him with a wave. "Axel is okay. He's just letting me know."

"Good. Tell him I wish him luck."

Rufus says good luck.

I'll need it, he replied. *This is going to be harder than I thought.*

Why?

I'll explain later. It's late. Get some rest. Stay away from Lacy.

I scoffed at that. *I love you.*

I love you. See you soon. Xoxo.

Xoxo.

"I've been thinking about your situation," Rufus said.

I slipped my phone back into my pocket and tipped my head toward him. "How's that?"

"I'm wondering if the dragon fire could help you create ice."

I frowned. "Seems like it would do the opposite."

"Perhaps, perhaps not." He stopped and scooped up a small stone. He palmed it as we continued. "Sometimes you need the opposite of a thing to push you forward. The opposite will spring forth from the very thing that it is the antithesis of."

"Fascinating," I said sarcastically.

He glared at me. "Your life is on the line."

I glanced down. Shame burned my cheeks. "I know. I'm sorry. Hermit told me today that basically I need to quit all the confusion in my life and then I'd be able to be focused enough to change the stone into ice." I smirked. "Do I really need a stone? Can't I just grab an ice cube and make it snow from that?"

Rufus chuckled. "You could, but I don't think it would be as effective."

"How do you mean?"

"The stone will hold more latent power. Let me show you."

Rufus plucked an ice cube from the sky. Like, literally he simply pulled it from nowhere—or everywhere, since we were talking about magic.

Once it was in his hand, Rufus spoke. "I can feel its energy. What the thing is capable of and this—is what it will do."

The ice cube shimmered and shook until it popped, transforming into a snowball.

Rufus handed the ball to me. "That's all it had within it. Now this"—he nodded to the stone—"is different. Its energy has never been used, unlike the ice, which was at one time water and then gas."

He capped a hand over the stone. "Let's see if I can do it."

Light shot out from under his hand. Rufus released the stone, and it exploded out. I shielded my eyes. When I pulled my hand away, a thousand snowflakes surrounded us, falling from the sky.

"Wow," I said in amazement. "That is cool."

"That is only the tip of the iceberg of the power inside that stone." A flake dropped into his open palm. "That's what you can do, Pepper. That and more."

I opened my hand, and a few wet, fluffy flakes drifted onto my skin. "You think Hugo may be able to help me?"

"He may." Rufus grabbed my arm. "We should get out of here. Any of the witches back there could've felt my magic. They could arrive any time."

"Then let's get out of here."

We scurried from the area, making sure we watched for sentries who were patrolling for people breaking curfew.

Yes, the curfew was still instated. I really, really didn't like Lacy.

We reached the house and found Betty sitting up, the guinea pig in her lap. She stroked its furry little body and whispered to it.

"You did good tonight, little Stevie."

I frowned. "Little Stevie?"

Betty nodded. "That's what I named him."

I shot Rufus a concerned look. He simply shrugged. "Stevie seems as good a name as any."

"How'd he do good?" I said.

Betty's mouth quirked into smile. She pulled a wand out from beside her. "He brought me this."

The dark wood wasn't anything special. The thing could've been a child's play toy except for one thing—poison ivy snaked around the bark.

I gasped. "That's Lacy's wand. How did you get it?"

Betty nodded down to Stevie. "He got it for me. Without this, she'll have much less of a chance to beat you in the competition."

I clapped with glee. "Oh, this is wonderful. So great, y'all."

Rufus frowned. "I wouldn't be so sure of that. Sometimes wands without their owners can be sneaky little beasts."

"Huh?" I said.

He pointed a finger at the wand. "I'd stay clear of it if I were you."

I smirked. Rufus knew a lot, but maybe he was wrong about this. "Anyway, Betty. We're looking for Hugo. Is he in my room?"

Betty's face paled. Her expression soured.

"What is it?" I said.

"They came," was all she said.

I bit down the panic fighting to scramble up my throat. "Who came?"

"Lacy and some others."

I gripped the back of the couch. "Why did they come?"

She stared at the floor. "For him. For Hugo."

"Are you saying they took him? Why?"

Her lower lip trembled. "Lacy said since they suspected the dragon of helping murder Bee, they were taking him with them."

I closed my eyes tightly. "Did they say what they would do to Hugo?"

Betty shook her head. "No, they did not." A glimmer of mischief shone in her eyes. She nodded to the guinea pig. "But I'm guessing we could find out."

THIRTEEN

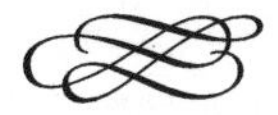

With Lacy's blatant stealing of Hugo, I was ticked. The first thing I wanted to know, of course, was whether or not he was safe.

According to Betty, Stevie would find that out for us. Rufus said he would work on that as well. But in the meantime it was late. Betty and I sat by the fire with Cordelia and Amelia, who had both come down from upstairs.

"What is that?" Amelia said, eyeing the wand.

"It's Lacy's wand," Cordelia said.

Amelia's jaw dropped. "When she figures out you've got it, she's going to rip our house to shreds."

Betty waved her hand dismissively. "She won't find out."

"If we can keep it away from her, then Lacy won't be able to beat me in the competition," I said.

"Isn't that cheating?" Amelia pointed out.

"It's giving Pepper an advantage," Betty said.

Cordelia picked up an apple lying in a fruit bowl and took a big bite. "Y'all aren't discussing the most obvious thing."

"Shouldn't you be rationing?" Amelia pointed out.

Cordelia ignored her. "Isn't Lacy going to notice that her wand is missing?"

"I've got a plan for that," Betty said. "I'll sneak a fake into her pocket tomorrow."

Cordelia stared blankly at Betty. "That sounds like a deadly idea."

"Or stupid," I added. "How are you going to slip it into her pocket?"

"I'm not." Betty grinned wickedly. "One of y'all will."

Needless to say, that didn't exactly go over well. None of us volunteered, but Betty wasn't disheartened. That was obvious from the devilish gleam in her eye.

She'd really grabbed hold of this whole resistance thing and had run with it.

The four of us headed off toward our bedrooms. Stevie followed me. I guess the guinea pig could tell that I was lonely.

Mattie the Cat greeted us when we entered. "Ooh, looks like supper."

Stevie froze. I scooped the rodent into my arms. "He's off-limits."

Mattie's tail flickered in annoyance. "I was only joking, sugar. Everyone knows guinea pigs are tough and stringy."

I gently placed Stevie on the bed. "You'll be fine here. She won't bother you."

Then I set off to shower and change my clothes. By the time I'd finished, both animals were sound asleep and I wasn't too far behind.

I awoke to a bright and sunny morning. I yawned widely, stretched my arms over my head and glanced at my phone to see if Axel had sent me any texts.

Morning, sunshine, he'd written.

Morning, yourself. I added a smiley face.

I laid the phone down beside me and noticed that Stevie was gone. I pushed up, searching for him, and did not expect to find him squatting at the foot of my bed.

Beside him lay Lacy's wand and—an eyeball!

I bolted up, biting back a scream. An eye! My gaze darted from the shiny blue iris to Stevie.

What sort of guinea pig was this? Some crazy carnivorous rodent that ate people? Because the eye was clearly human.

A quick search of the room revealed no Mattie. "Where's my cat?" I demanded.

Mattie sauntered from the bathroom. "I'm right here."

I pointed at the orb, trying to keep my voice calm. "Did you see that?"

Mattie blinked at the objects. She yawned. "What? That glass eye?"

My rising panic dissipated. "It's *glass?*"

The cat strode over and batted it from the rug. It hit the wooden floor with a *thunk.*

I exhaled and sank back onto the bed. "Oh, thank goodness. I thought…"

"That the rodent had killed someone?"

When she put it that way, I had to grudgingly admit it sounded ridiculous.

"Of course I didn't think that," I scoffed. "How ludicrous." I reached down and patted Stevie. He leaned into my hand, so I scratched him behind the ears.

"But whose eye is it?" Mattie said.

Then I remembered that Rufus had mentioned that Widdon wore a glass eye. I groaned. The last thing I wanted to do was hand some crime lord his eye. That would put a lot of unwanted attention on me. Let's face it, I already had enough attention—the bad kind.

But at the same time it would give me an excuse to speak with him, find out what he knew, if anything, about Bee's death. If I could rule out the three witches vying for her old position, I could then focus on Lacy as the killer.

Which made the most sense to me anyway seeing as she was one nasty witch.

I was apprehensive about touching the eye but had no choice. Cringing, I plucked it from the wood. The smooth surface was cool in my fingers.

I considered the fact that a head witch would have a glass eye as opposed to healing himself. I wondered if there was a story there.

Figuring there wasn't time to delve into the mysteries of head witches, I dressed and picked up the wand, eyeball and Stevie, who might have to start being locked up at night so that he didn't run away. I would mention it to Betty, but had a feeling that would screw with her whole "resistance movement" plans.

I grabbed the doorknob and turned, or at least tried to turn. The knob wouldn't give.

I gritted my teeth and gave it a stronger tug. Darned thing still wouldn't move.

"Okay," I shouted, "whose big idea was it to lock me in?"

Amelia's voice came from the other side. "It wasn't me. Pretty sure it wasn't Cordelia."

"What's all this ruckus?" Grandma Betty said.

"I'm locked in." I pulled the door. "It won't budge."

Betty paused. "Is that wand in there with you?"

I stared down at it. "Yes."

"That's it. Silly thing is playing a trick."

The wand looked innocent as I gripped it. "Can you fix this, Betty? I've got to get out of here."

Just then the wand zipped from my hand and hovered in the air. It moved left and right, thrusting out sprays of magic. One of the tendrils hit my mirror. A flame burst from the mirror.

I screeched. "It's setting my room on fire!"

It zapped the bed with another flame. The wand danced around, seeming to laugh at me.

"You're not mischievous," I snarled. "You're just plain old evil."

I dashed to the window and threw it open. "Mattie, get Stevie out of here."

Mattie's yellow eyes widened in fear. "What are you gonna do, sugar? Fight it?"

I rolled up my sleeves. "I dang sure am."

From the other side of the door I heard Betty and my cousins yelling, trying to get the door open.

I whirled on the wand. It stopped mid-dance. It was like the two of us were staring down one another. Smoke started filling the room. I coughed as the caustic fumes irritated my lungs and made my throat burn.

"You will stop," I demanded.

The wand twirled away and sent another flaming finger to ignite one of my blouses.

"That's my best shirt!"

Hence the reminder to always pick my clothes up and leave them in the closet. Perhaps I should start being neater.

I focused my magic on making the wand breaking in two. I had to stop the thing somehow.

But it didn't work. Then I realized that I was doing it all wrong.

This was a fire wand. It possessed elemental power. I had to fight one element with another.

My gaze darted around the room. What could I use? The smoke thickened, making it harder to breath, and the heat—it was oppressive.

I grabbed a damp towel from last night's shower. I begged, I wished and I pleaded for the thing to turn into ice.

Nothing happened.

Then I thought about Axel, that I would never see him again. That he was all alone in the sticks. Emotion unfurled in my chest like a great ribbon flowing from me. The towel in my hand started to transform.

It became a sheet of liquid that I threw at the wand. Every fire in my room was quenched as the wall of water enveloped the poison-ivy-covered stick, wrapping it in a magical cocoon.

The wand fell limply to the floor, and the door burst open. Betty and my cousins stood staring at my room. Smoke churned on the ceiling. Betty clapped her hands. A breeze whisked the fumes out the window.

"What happened?" Betty said.

I stared at the wand and the towel. A slow smile curled on my face. "I guess I learned how to tap into my powers to transform one thing into an element. Granted, it wasn't the element I wanted, but it worked."

The wand wriggled under the towel. Betty slowly bent over and scooped the struggling wand into her arms. "I think I'll have to find a better container to hold it in."

Cordelia smirked. "You sure you don't want to just give it back?"

Betty smiled mysteriously. "Nope. Not yet."

Betty made sure all the fires were completed quenched. She then righted my bedroom, even saving my blouse from the ashes. She was also nice enough to get rid of the smoke smell from my clothes and hair.

When we got downstairs, Rufus was waiting.

"Good news," I said. "I changed a towel into a wall of water."

"That is good news," he said proudly.

"Bad news is I was trying to turn it into ice."

He nodded in understanding. "One step at a time."

"But there's more good news."

He hiked a brow in question. "What would that be?"

I flashed the eyeball. "Got this little diddy from Stevie. I think it belongs to Widdon Franks."

"Let me see that."

I handed it to him. Rufus turned it right and left and finally palmed it in his hand. "So it does." A slow smile curled on his lips. "Let's go see if he needs it back."

FOURTEEN

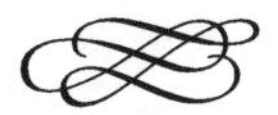

Ever since the mass of head witches had entered town, they had converged on the few restaurants we had for their meals. Since Spellin' Skillet was the best place around for comfort food and since Widdon was, well, let's put it this way—huge—it seemed Spellin' would be the place to find him.

Rufus and I arrived right at the lunch rush. We had to wait for a table, which gave me plenty of time to search for the ex–crime lord.

I nodded to a four-top clear in back. "He's back there."

Widdon faced us. This close I could see his second chin resting on his third and fourth chins that spread like butter onto his chest.

I nudged Rufus. "Tell him you want to have a meeting."

He scoffed. "Is that your grand plan?"

"Okay, tell him I'm a huge fan of his."

He rolled his eyes.

I shrugged. "Well then I'll do it." I strode off.

Rufus caught up to me. "Do you know what you're doing?"

"No, of course not," I snapped. "But we have to do something. We've got a dead witch, a town on lockdown and an insane woman who wants to ooze my powers from me and leave me a vegetable." I glared at him. "So yes, I'm going in."

"Okay," Rufus relented. "But let me lead."

I grinned at him. "Absolutely."

We reached the table, and Rufus extended his hand. "Widdon Franks, I'm Rufus Mayes. Pleased to meet you."

The wizard sitting across from Widdon got up and left. Widdon himself wore an eye patch over his missing organ. I palmed the glass object in my pocket.

Gross, huh? I never would've done it if the eye had been real, but glass was different and it was clean. There wasn't any goop on it.

Ew. I recoiled at the thought of goop.

Rufus gestured to the open bench seat. "May we join you?"

Widdon eyed me. "You're Pepper Dunn. It might not be wise for me to be seen with you in public."

I clicked my tongue. "Oh? Fraternizing with the enemy and all that?"

Widdon wiped his plump sausage fingers on a napkin. "Something like that," he said in a deep voice. "You might be bad for business."

"I'm not looking to buy anything from you. I'm not interested in black market offerings."

Widdon's eyes narrowed.

Rufus whispered, "Pepper," in warning.

Okay, so maybe I shouldn't have brought up that I knew he had been a crime lord. But really—what did I have to lose?

Not one thing.

Widdon's face cracked into a smile. "You're a dame with gonads. I like you. Sit."

Rufus and I sat before the kingpin—or ex, as it was.

"What can I do for you?"

"We're looking for information," Rufus said.

"I don't give anything without getting something in return."

I nearly rolled my eyes. Of course he didn't. "I have something of yours—something you'll want back."

He quirked the only brow I could see. "That is?"

I glanced at Rufus, who nodded slightly. I pulled the eye from my pocket and laid it on the table.

Widdon practically salivated at the sight of it—no pun intended. "How'd you get your mitts on my eye?"

Did I mention he also spoke like a gangster?

"Never mind," I said curtly. "But I've got it and I'm more than willing to give it back." I flipped a strand of red hair from my shoulders. "For a price."

"A dame who drives a hard bargain. It's a shame you won't join us."

"I'm not into harming werewolves. I'm partial to them."

He shrugged. "Sometimes you have to take what's yours, no matter the price."

Widdon studied me with his one good eye. A shudder threatened to zip down my spine. I shook it off.

Rufus steered the conversation back to the matter at hand. "We need to know why you want to be one of the three."

Widdon cracked a smile. "Why? You voting?"

"No, but a witch is dead—one who was trying to help me," I snapped.

His expression sobered. "The position became available, and let's just say I don't like to waste opportunities."

"It's close to getting into the High Witch Council," I said.

"A few steps away," Widdon said. "The Order needs strong leadership. That's why I tossed my hat in the ring. Bee was kind—too kind; it's probably what got her killed."

"Did you know her well?" I said.

"Well enough that I could tell she'd end up dying trying to save someone who wasn't worth it," he said smugly. Widdon picked up a fry from his plate and dredged it through a pond of ketchup before eating it.

"She was burned," I said. "It's a horrible way to die."

"It's how witches have been killed for centuries," Widdon remarked. "But if you're really asking if I killed her or knew anything about her death—no, I didn't. The only thing I can tell you is that in order to make it out of the camp the way she did to meet you, she would've had to have either slipped past a guard or paid them off."

Widdon eyed me. "My bet would be that she paid someone off. Bee might've been one of the three, but she wasn't top dog when it came to magic. In my opinion that's one of the reasons she wound up dead."

"Who were the guards on duty that night?" Rufus asked.

Widdon opened his palm. "The eye first."

I grabbed it. "No. First you tell us who was on guard."

Widdon smiled, but his eye held no warmth for me. "I'll tell you who the most important one was."

"And who was that?"

"Young fella," Widdon said, "named Sherman Oaks."

"Isn't he vying to be one of the three?" I said to Rufus.

Rufus nodded. "Yes, he is."

I extended my hand and dropped the eye into Widdon's palm. "Thanks for your help. If we need anything else, can we talk to you?"

Widdon flipped up the pirate patch and shoved the glass eye in its socket. "Of course. But don't forget"—he smiled smugly—"I don't give nothin' away for free. Everything comes with a price."

Rufus rose and I followed. I glared down at Widdon, a man who had bartered in the underworld.

I placed both of my palms on the table and leaned over, glaring at him. "I know, Mr. Franks. You can't get something for nothing. But at some point have you ever asked yourself if the price you paid was worth it?"

His jaw dropped, and I turned to Rufus. "Let's go."

Once we were out of earshot, Rufus whirled on me. "You must be joking to have asked an ex-kingpin if the price he paid was worth it. Are you trying to get us killed?"

"No," I scoffed. "Of course not. I just didn't want him to think he held all the power. It annoyed me."

Rufus cursed at the sky. "Well, at least we have a bit of information about Sherman."

"Well, Pepper Dunn, looking to become one of us?"

Lacy's acrid voice sliced through every other conversation in the room.

I stopped, contemplating whether I should justify her with conversation or simply keep walking.

I decided I wasn't rolling over for any witch—especially not her.

I pivoted on my heel and faced her. Lacy sat at a large round table, looking like she was holding court in Spellin' Skillet.

"No, I wasn't looking to become one of you. Become someone who takes whatever she wants and hurts people along the way? Wait, not hurt, *destroy,* like you did to that one head witch—the one who became a vegetable after she dealt with you? No, I would rather die than have that happen to me."

Lacy sneered. "That can be arranged."

I fisted my hands. "I will be ready for you. But I warn you, Lacy, you're messing with the wrong witch."

Lacy threw back her head and cackled. "An untrained head witch is going to tell me that I'm messing with the wrong witch?" Her mouth became a grim line. "You have a lot of nerve."

Suddenly something long and thin slipped into my hand. I glanced down and saw a replica of Lacy's poison ivy wand. I scanned the room for Betty, but of course she was nowhere to be found. How the heck was I supposed to slip the stupid wand into Lacy's pocket without her knowing?

The answer hit me like a load of hay. I pulled the wand from behind my back.

Lacy's eyes widened. "How did you—"

I peered down at her and pulled my lips back into a sneer. "I would watch who you call untrained."

I handed her the wand, nodded to Rufus and said, "Let's go."

Without another word, I pivoted on my heels and stomped from the restaurant.

"You learned something today."

Hermit and I stood in the Conjuring Caverns. The lantern sat on the floor, the light spinning inside. Shadows danced around the cave, dappling the walls with cutouts of broomsticks, half-moons and unicorn horns.

"I'm more interested in finding out where my dragon is," I said, "than discussing whatever I learned."

"He's safe," Hermit said quietly. "The dragon will not be harmed."

I raked my fingers through my hair. "How can I be sure of that?"

"If Lacy were to harm your familiar openly, that would cause a large disturbance not only within the Order but also in your community."

"But taking my powers is fine," I said bitterly.

"People get upset when animals are hurt. That's why animals don't die in movies." He rubbed his hands as if to warm them. "You could join her. That is the other option."

"Never."

Hermit nodded. "But as I was saying, you learned something today."

"What's that?"

He laughed. "You're the one who told me you changed the towel into a wall of water."

I sighed and sank onto the floor, crossing my legs in front of me. "Yes, I did say that. Sorry. It's been very stressful lately. I know my true power is connected to love and fear."

"It's connected to clear thinking," Hermit added. "Before, you weren't thinking clearly. You have…distractions."

I closed my eyes tightly and said words I had to force out. "You mean Rufus."

He nodded. "I do."

I fisted my hands and opened my eyes. "I don't understand it. I never have. But I have feelings for him. Not like Axel, though. Not even close. Axel owns my heart, but Rufus seems to just be standing on the outside as a temptation. The time of being wishy-washy is over. Staying in the mire for too long makes me unable to move forward."

"No one can move forward when stuck, my dear."

I nodded in understanding. "And that's what I've been—stuck. I've been foolish, thinking that if I pushed certain parts of my life away, I could ignore them and things would work out for themselves. What

I've realized is that I need to give myself over to fate and love and stop worrying about *what-ifs,* and also stop being so darned childish."

I rubbed my temples. "It's because of me that the entire town is in this predicament. If I'd only learned how to use my powers earlier, we wouldn't be here. The Order wouldn't have overtaken us, and my town wouldn't be on lockdown. We could leave. Food could enter. I only hope this town's patience lasts long enough for me to defeat Lacy. Because if they turn on me before that...well, I couldn't say I blamed them."

Hermit inhaled deeply. "It is a lot you have on your shoulders. You remind me of myself, my dear. When I was your age, I had so much power. Yet I was young, stupid with it. There were those who needed my help and in my haughtiness I believed they should have been able to help themselves, so I did nothing. Doing nothing was the worst possible outcome. Because of me, innocent people suffered, so I understand your plight."

"Hermit," I said cautiously, "why are you helping me?"

He cocked his head to one side. "Because you should be given a chance to fight, and because I suppose I'm paying penance for my mistakes. I don't want to see an innocent suffer. I didn't want to turn away again. I wanted to help."

"But why didn't you help the werewolves instead of me? Convince Lacy to speak to the wolves and figure out the situation?"

He chuckled. "Because she wouldn't have listened, and there's too much ingrained prejudice against them for things to be so simple."

He clapped his hands. "Now. Are you ready for your lesson?"

I rose and brushed dirt from the seat of my pants. "Yes, I am. But Hermit?"

"Yes, my dear?"

"What happened? To those people who you regret not helping?"

Hermit stared at the shapes as they danced and spiraled on the wall. After a moment he answered.

"They all died."

FIFTEEN

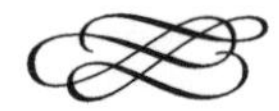

My training with Hermit went about as well as the day before. The occurrence with the blanket of water wasn't repeated, even though I tried.

I wasn't sure what the problem was. Hermit suggested it wasn't a focus problem, but apparently some things still had to click together that hadn't already.

When I got home, it was close to supper. I said hello to everyone and headed upstairs to collect my thoughts before I went back down to eat.

As soon as I reached my room, my phone rang.

Axel.

My hands shook as I thumbed the phone on and pressed it to my ear.

"Axel?"

"Hey, babe, how are you?"

I sank onto the bed. "Better now that I've heard your voice. How's it going?"

"I'm finding my way in. You wouldn't believe how hard it is down here to get a meeting with the alpha in the pack."

I rolled my eyes. "It's gotta be better down there than it is here. Every time I run into Lacy, she reminds me that I'm dead meat."

"Don't say that," he said sharply.

"Sorry." I sighed and lay back on the mattress. "But seriously, I've made some strides in my magic, and Betty stole Lacy's wand."

"Did she? And is your grandmother still alive to tell the tale?"

I chuckled. "So far. But I did have an encounter with the wand. Lucky for me I managed to figure out how to stop it—and made a breakthrough with my magic in the process."

"That's fantastic," he said proudly. "What happened?"

I told him all about it. He listened quietly, and when I was finished, he said, "But you weren't able to replicate it today?"

"No," I said, annoyed. "I know I can do it. It's the key to defeating Lacy. I have to be able to stop her, Axel."

"I'm hoping to be finished here tomorrow or the next day. I should be back before you clash with her."

I gripped the phone with both hands. How I wanted to fling my arms around Axel's neck and hug him tight. I missed him so much my heart ached.

I brushed away a tear that had leaked from my eye. "I wish you would return now. Axel, I've thought about your proposal and I want to answer."

"No," he insisted. "Not until we're face-to-face. I won't have an answer over a phone call. It's not right."

"You didn't even give me a ring," I reminded him. "It's not like this whole thing has been incredibly traditional."

"Just because I didn't have a ring before doesn't mean I don't have one now," he said.

My breath caught in my throat. "Oh," was all I could think of to say. "Well, then."

"So let's wait." His voice sounded husky. "I'll be back soon. Just don't get too comfortable with Rufus while I'm gone."

My gut twisted. "Axel, about him…"

"What?" he growled. "Did he make a move on you?"

I shook my head. "No, of course not. Listen, I want to be honest with you."

"About your feelings for him."

I closed my eyes and sat up. "You know."

"I'm not a fool," he said. "But I also know that whatever bond you have with him, it doesn't compare to us. Never has. Never will. He can be good as much as he wants. Rufus's core may change, but he's watery, mercurial. When he wants to be good, he will be. But if something changed and he decided to return to a life of destruction, then he would do that without any regard for you."

Axel sighed. "I know that isn't what you want to hear, but I believe that's the truth. When it comes to your bond with him, something happened when he placed the spell on you that married your power to his. I think Rufus was able to see good in you and want that. He wanted to change *for you,* Pepper. Not for anyone else, not even for himself. You've helped him in a way I don't even think Rufus understands. That's what your bond is with him. It's two people who shared a connection and who possibly wanted more. But can you both exist in the other's world?"

"No," I answered. Agony filled me. I didn't know how much, if any, of this hurt Axel, and to be honest, I didn't want to ask. Yes, I was afraid of the truth.

"I had to learn that for myself," I said. "Figure out that my true feelings are with you. I mean, I've always known that," I added quickly, "but there were times, like when you were gone, when you broke up with me and left. Rufus helped me—helped this town."

"And I'm glad for that," Axel said. "He did what he should have. For once it was the right thing."

I smiled. "I'm so glad you called."

I could practically hear the giant grin forming on his face. "Me too. If anything changes or Lacy decides to move quickly, call me. I'll leave everything to be there."

"I will, but Betty's got the resistance going and hopefully that'll keep the Order busy enough that they won't be too concerned with me—at least for a little while."

"And what about Bee's killer?"

"I still think it's Lacy, but need proof. Oh, she took Hugo."

"What?"

I cringed. "I know. I've heard he's okay, but I haven't seen him."

"Pepper, she did that to ruin your chances of defeating her. You've got to get him back."

Now I was getting worried. If Axel was worried, that meant I should be, too. "How? I don't even know where he is."

He sighed angrily. "Use your family. They'll help."

"Thanks," I said weakly.

"And Pepper?"

"Yes?"

"I love you."

I practically melted into the phone. "I love you, too."

We hung up. I lay on the bed for several minutes, recuperating. Finally I went downstairs to find a meal of chicken and dumplings, pinto beans and cornbread.

Talk about starch city. After I finished that meal, I'd be lucky if someone could roll me away from the table.

I took a seat across from Betty. "How's the wand?"

"It's stable. I've been able to encase it in glass," my grandmother replied. "That seems to stop it from doing any nasty tricks."

Amelia pointed her fork at Betty. "I told her she should give it to me and I'll take it to the Vault."

"That might be the most sane idea you've ever had," Cordelia said.

Amelia shot her a dark look. "You're just jealous that you didn't come up with it first."

Cordelia rolled her eyes.

"What's going on at the wish store?"

Cordelia's father was half-genie and had expressed his interest in opening a shop. Cordelia planned on leaving her position at the inn to take a job with him.

Cordelia shook her head. "As soon as the Order came into town, they put the shop on hold."

"Yeah, it's too bad we couldn't wish our way out of this," Amelia said sadly.

I thought about that for a minute. "It's too bad. What I'd rather wish for is to know the identity of Bee's killer. Oh, and have Axel put this stupid witch/werewolf conflict to rest."

Amelia patted my hand. "He'll do the best he can."

"Or," I said, still thinking about it, "could I wish for Sherman Oaks to arrive so I can ask him about Bee? It seems he might've seen her the night she was killed."

"How about you just wish to have Lacy swept into a parallel universe?" Amelia offered. "Out of all the possible outcomes, that seems like the best."

Cordelia pointed her attention at Betty. "Do you think she's going to figure out you stole her wand?"

Betty grimaced. "I'm relying on the fact that she won't need it until she faces off with Pepper and when she doesn't have it, Pepper easily defeats her."

I rolled my eyes. "Yeah, sounds like a perfectly ridiculous plan. You've got to come up with something better, because I can almost guarantee that Lacy will discover her wand is gone. Since I handed her the dummy, she'll come looking for me. Thanks for that one, Betty," I said sarcastically.

Stevie, who'd been sitting beside me at the foot of the table, suddenly jumped up and scurried toward the door. He pawed at the base.

"You gotta go potty, little guy?" I wiped dumpling residue from my mouth and crossed over. I opened the door for him, and Stevie scampered into the night.

"Huh, guess he really had to go," I murmured.

Thunder echoed in the sky. The air contracted and shifted. The barometric pressure changed, and the atmosphere thickened with humidity.

"Uh-oh," Betty said.

I turned to her. "What?"

"That isn't an ordinary storm."

I frowned. "What is it, then?"

A voice crackled from a bolt of lightning that splintered across the sky. "Who stole my wand?"

I groaned. "Well, I guess the cat's out of the bag about the wand."

"She's discovered us." Betty hopped from her seat. "Amelia, I need your help. You must hide Lacy's wand in the Vault."

Amelia's eyes flared. "Now you want me to hide it? Now, when she's going to be looking for it? Uh-huh. That woman will kill me if she discovers I took it."

Betty smiled. "But you didn't take it. I did."

Amelia rolled her eyes. "I don't think that's going to matter. If I get caught with it, I'm dead meat."

The voice boomed from the sky. "Your houses will be searched! All of them. Whoever has taken my wand will pay dearly! The Order has been kind to you people of Magnolia Cove, but no more!"

I knew Lacy wasn't joking. We would be dead—all of us, if she found the wand here. Amelia didn't want to take it, but what other choice did we have?

I stepped toward Betty. "I'll do it. I'll take the wand."

Amelia gasped. "Pepper, you can't. If Lacy finds you…"

"If she finds the thing here, we're dead. It won't matter. I have to do this. It must be moved."

Cordelia rose. "I'll go with you. Since Amelia's too chicken to help, I'll be the cousin who rises to the occasion."

"I'm not chicken," Amelia fumed. "I just was being careful is all."

Thunder rocked the sky, and lightning splintered the night. "We have to hurry. The Order will arrive any minute, y'all. Betty, where's the wand?"

Betty clapped her hands, and a glass tube with the poison ivy wand appeared. The wand clinked against its prison, obviously trying to find a way out.

"Can you hide it at the Vault, Amelia?" I said. "It's pretty testy."

She nibbled her bottom lip. "I'll try."

Another clap of thunder echoed outside. I grabbed a rain jacket from a hook. "We'd better get going."

Cordelia snapped her fingers, and she and Amelia were outfitted with rain jackets and boots. She cracked her knuckles. "Come on. Let's get out of here before Lacy and her goons show up."

Amelia peered hesitantly outside. "It's curfew. Do you think we'll make it?"

I zipped up my jacket and tucked the wand under my arm. "We have no choice. Our lives are on the line."

"In that case"—Amelia pulled up her hood defiantly—"let's get going."

SIXTEEN

The wind blew hard through town. I considered that lucky since the wand was beating itself senseless against the glass container.

"That thing sure is temperamental," Amelia said.

I nodded. "That's one reason we need to get it somewhere safe. I don't know what Betty was thinking stealing it."

"She could've gotten us all killed," Cordelia griped. "Her and that stupid resistance of hers."

"Hey," Amelia said defensively, "it's not stupid. She's doing it to protect us."

"She put us in more danger," Cordelia snapped. "Here we are, outside after curfew, delivering this thing to the Vault—where you work, might I remind you. If Erasmus Everlasting finds out you've hidden contraband, he'll be ticked. You'll be in trouble. Fired at the least. Who the heck knows what'll happen that's worse than firing—imprisonment?"

Amelia stopped. "Maybe we should just risk the Order." She turned around and started to head back to the house. Cordelia and I both hooked our arms around her elbows.

"Stop it," I said. "Cordelia's overreacting. Aren't you, Cord?"

My cousin rolled her eyes. "Yes, I'm overreacting. None of those bad things will happen to you, so don't worry."

Cordelia had led us down our block. We were circling the neighborhood. Basically taking the long way to the Vault. It wasn't a route I was familiar with, but it looked like up ahead there was a grove of dogwood trees.

"Those are so pretty," I whispered.

Cordelia motioned for us to stop. We did. She glanced right and left and then at the trees. "This is the least likely route that Lacy and the Order will take to search the town. It's out of the way and no houses."

"Yeah," I said, "why not take it? It's so pretty."

"Because of the barking dogwoods," Cordelia said.

I frowned. "I'm sorry?"

"The trees," Amelia clarified. "They bark."

I stared at my cousins in surprise. "And I'm only just hearing about this now?"

"Like I said," Cordelia added, "no one lives over here because of that. The trees can be loud, but we've got the thunder overhead and the fact that the Order should be a little bit behind us. It should be okay."

I stared at the seemingly quiet trees skeptically. "To do what?"

"To cross through."

"So we're going to march through that grove, hope the trees don't bark so loud they catch crazy Lacy's attention, and haul butt to the Vault?"

Cordelia exhaled. "That sounds about right."

I nodded. "Then let's go."

Amelia grabbed my hand. "They're asleep now. But at the first sign that they're going to bark, we need to run as fast as we can."

Cordelia nodded. "They're loud, and even over the storm they might be heard."

"Okay," I said.

The three of us clasped hands. I'd tucked the wand under my arm. It jutted out but was secure.

The grass was soft under my feet. The wind howled and thunder still clapped overhead but it was focused more toward the houses in town.

White and pink dogwood blossoms swayed in the wind. They were lovely as moonlight cast its luminescence over them. I wanted to reach out and touch the velvety petals, but I knew better.

"They're so pretty," Amelia whispered. "I just want to feel them."

"No," Cordelia snapped. "They're enchanted, Amelia. You know that. Don't touch them!"

Amelia blinked. She shook her head. "You're right. I'm sorry. I lost myself."

"Stay focused," Cordelia said.

We trudged through, walking as quietly as possible. Several times we had to wedge ourselves between trees, holding our breath so we wouldn't brush up against them.

"Almost through," Cordelia whispered. "Just a few more steps."

Something scurried over Amelia's foot. She released my hand, threw up her arms and screamed.

The nearest dogwood tree reared back. The center of its trunk twisted into a snout, like an animal's—or a dog's, to be more precise—and half a breath later, a piercing bark splintered the night.

Suddenly the other dogwoods roared to life, barking and yipping. It was loud. It was earsplitting.

"Run," I yelled.

The three of us hightailed it through the barking dogwoods. We were almost to the edge, where the grove stopped.

I glanced back in time to see a dozen witches from the Order's ranks descend on the trees.

They would see us. We would be found. I had to do something. I yanked my cousins to a stop.

"What?" Cordelia said.

"We can't run. They'll find us."

Amelia cringed. "What do we do?"

A wave of power flowed through me. Light engulfed the three of us. My hands elongated to branches, my torso became thick and hard and my breathing stilled.

The same happened to my cousins. I watched as their faces disappeared, becoming longs strips of bark attached to magically created trees.

The witches had been far enough away that they hadn't seen the transformation. We were anchored to a spot thick with trees. The witches flew quickly, scouring the area within seconds.

If we'd reached the tree line, where it opened up to the Vault, we would've been discovered for sure.

Wizards and witches darted through the dogwoods, calling to one another and trying to coax out whoever had caused such a stir.

I held my breath when Lacy's face popped up in front of me. "These three trees are strange," she murmured.

"They're exactly like the others," another witch said.

"I didn't say they were different," Lacy snapped. "I said they were strange."

The witch scoffed. "The same sort of strange you think that Betty Craple is?"

"That old woman is up to something. We didn't find my wand with her, but I have a feeling she knows more than what she's saying."

"Half of the dimwit witches in this town do," the witch said. I finally recognized her as Slug, who was running to take Bee's open spot as one of the three. "If they only realized all of this is for show. It doesn't matter what they want or how much they think they've got Pepper Dunn safe. No matter, you're going to take what you want."

"I know." Lacy giggled. "Bee was so stupid to think she could outsmart me. That she could keep things hidden. Of course I knew she was going to meet Pepper and try to help her."

Lacy threw back her head and laughed. "It didn't matter, though, did it? She wound up dead, and we'll have a new witch in her place. Hopefully someone who understands what it really means to be one of the three."

"Poor pathetic little Sherman," Slug said. "He doesn't stand a chance. He thinks he's living up to what his mother wanted by taking her place. He's so stupid."

Wait. *What?*

What an avalanche of information. Sherman was Bee's son. Lacy was going to take me no matter what—that wasn't exactly a revelation, I suppose. I knew that. I just had to find a way to stop her—*really* stop her.

Lacy wanted Slug to take Bee's place. Did that mean Lacy had set everything up?

Gosh, it would be too easy if Lacy simply admitted to it, wouldn't it? I mean, why couldn't she just save me a ton of trouble and say, *I did it. I killed Bee.*

"Where's Sherman tonight?" Lacy said. "You're in charge of him."

"He's over by the Potion Ponds, guarding the place." Slug threw back her head and laughed. "He's out there while I'm over here, proving how much better I'd be at being one of y'all." She threw her thick, luscious hair over one shoulder. "He's such a moron, he didn't even realize I was making him look bad when I gave him the assignment."

Lacy shivered. "Come on. Let's go. There's nothing in these woods. It was a false alarm."

Slug stopped right in front of me. She stared at my bark as if trying to see into it. "I think you're right, Lacy. There does seem to be something strange about these trees."

She wore a pointy conical like every stereotypical wicked witch wore in movies and cartoons. Slug pulled a long hatpin from the brim and moved to poke me.

"Come on," Lacy said. "Don't waste a poke on that tree. Use it somewhere else."

Slug pushed the pin back into her hat. As the two witches walked away, an idea popped into my head.

If I'd had lips, they would've coiled into a smile. Well, well, well, it looked like Sherman Oaks might end up being our best ally in this thing yet.

~

WE TUCKED the wand safely into the Vault, and Cordelia worked a binding spell to reinforce the glass case.

"Hope that works," Amelia muttered. "Otherwise I'll be in deep crap."

Cordelia scoffed. "Erasmus will never even know you put it here. Don't worry. It'll be fine."

Amelia shook her head. "I'm pretty sure the words 'don't worry' have come before all major tragedies in the world."

I elbowed Amelia. "I think what she means is there's no point in worrying. Come on. I've got an adventure for us."

"That was enough adventure for one night."

"Oh no," I said, "we need one more. We've got to go talk to Sherman Oaks."

Amelia's eyes widened. "He's in the Order."

"And he's being betrayed. He'll want to know."

Cordelia clapped a hand on Amelia's shoulder. "What's the worst that could happen?"

Amelia rubbed her face. "Once again, words that come before great tragedy."

I smiled widely. "Come on. Let's go."

We reached the Potion Ponds a few minutes later. Sherman Oaks stood at the edge staring into the glittering water. He looked like he was contemplating his life.

As he pondered that, Sherman took a couple of steps, tripping over his feet and nearly landing headfirst in the pond. He rose, brushed himself off and shook out his robes.

Sherman fixed his hair and whirled around as if to make sure no one had seen his embarrassing moment.

Cordelia cracked a smile. "This is going to be fun."

"Follow my lead," I said.

I strode out from a giant blooming azalea bush and whistled. Sherman jumped in my direction, his hands poised to karate chop me.

"Who's there? Don't come any closer. There's a curfew."

Having already figured out that I could work magical circles around this guy, I didn't bother listening to his warning.

"Hi, Sherman. I'm Pepper Dunn, and these are my cousins, Amelia and Cordelia."

Sherman studied us with suspicion in his eyes. "I could have you arrested. Lacy wants you."

"Correction: Lacy wants my powers. Not me. I'm sorry about what happened to your mother."

Sherman's face darkened. "That's right! Pepper! It was your dragon that killed my mother."

He started to rush me. Cordelia raised her hand. Sherman stopped mid-run, frozen by my cousin.

"That's enough," she said. "My cousin didn't kill your mother."

"Oh yeah?" he said, straining against her power. "I don't believe you."

"Then believe this," I demanded. "A few minutes ago the three of us overheard Slug and Lacy talking about you—about how you running for your mother's vacant position is a joke. They're playing you, Sherman. You were sent out here to make it look like you don't care about being one of the three. They want to make it easy for Slug to defeat you."

Sherman's mouth twisted as if he was going to say something; then he shut it. When he opened it again, he spoke. "You're lying."

"She's not lying." Amelia walked right up to him and crossed her arms. "Now listen, I know my cousin has a lot going against her right now, but she's not a cotton-pickin' liar. None of us are. We don't care about you or your Order. Heck, we want y'all out of our town ASAP. But seeing as how Lacy's making a big stink of stealing my cousin's powers for some werewolf/witch skirmish when there's a ton of y'all who can fight, well, we just have to face off against her. We can't let her win. From what my cousin says, your mama didn't want Lacy to win, either."

Sherman's eyes widened the more Amelia spoke. His gaze washed over her from head to foot before he finally said, "Yes, ma'am. You're right. I'm sorry. My mama, Bee, she did want you to be okay, Pepper. She was against Lacy's plan from the start."

I stepped forward and Amelia stepped away, but Sherman's gaze trailed after her. "I saw you and your mother arguing the day she died."

Sherman sighed. "She was starting to speak up against Lacy. I told her to be quiet, but she wouldn't hear of it. It may have been what got her killed." He sighed. "I'm sorry I said all that about your dragon. I know he didn't have anything to do with it. I know he was set up. It's obvious. Somebody else killed her. That's why I want her seat. I figured if I was in a more powerful position, I could figure out who the killer was."

Cordelia released the force field around him. Sherman rolled his shoulders. "Thanks." He pointed toward town. "But as y'all can see, I'm not in any sort of position to help. I got stuck out here, away from all the action. When Lacy discovered her wand was missing, I asked to hunt for it. I was told no."

"I'm sorry." I gave him an encouraging smile. "But I wanted you to know what we'd overheard."

Sherman shook his head. "It's pointless. They'll never let me be one of the three just the same as Lacy won't let you go—at least not alive."

I shuddered.

Amelia clapped her hands. "Then the two of y'all just need to figure out how to work together so that Sherman's mother's murderer is discovered, he takes her seat and Pepper is left safe and sound."

Sherman picked up a rock and tossed it into the pond. "I'm game. I am. Nothing could be worse than what they're having me do now, where I'm left by myself with no chance of having any leadership."

I rubbed my chin. "We have to come up with a plan."

"Sherman," Cordelia said, "how's your magic?"

He threw up his arms. "Awful. Horrible. I have two left feet when it comes to magic. I'm only part head witch, you see, and the only reason I'm in the Order is because of my mother."

Cordelia's mouth curled into a grin. "If you could wish for anything, would you wish to be a stronger wizard?"

Sherman exhaled a plume of air. "Would I ever!"

Amelia smiled. "Then we might be able to help you."

Another voice cut through the night. "I may be of service as well."

Rufus stepped out of the shadows.

"Rufus," I hissed. "How long have you been there?"

His lips coiled devilishly. "I've been around since the barking dogwoods."

"So you know everything." It almost annoyed me that Rufus was so flippant about having followed us, but at the same time I knew he would've protected me and my cousins if need be.

"I had to make sure you were safe." He turned his attention to Sherman. "And it looks like we've got a wizard to create. If we're going to make him powerful and have you beat Lacy, then we've got a lot of work to do."

I rubbed my hands together gleefully. I could practically feel the glint of mischief in my eye when I asked, "When do we start?"

SEVENTEEN

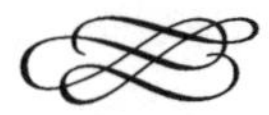

The best place we could figure out to help Sherman was none other than our house.

Betty was thrilled to add another member to her resistance. She was also excited to have another person to teach magic to. Since Sherman was only part head witch, Betty had given herself the job of tutor, which was fine by pretty much everyone except Sherman.

"Amelia, are you sure you can't teach me?" Sherman said the next day.

Amelia's eyelids fluttered. She scowled at the lopsided grin on his face. "I'm excellent at magic, but I wouldn't be a great tutor."

"Oh? Why not?"

"I don't have the patience," she said pertly.

Sherman's expression fell. Cordelia cleared her throat. "I have a surprise for you, Sherman, something that should help you with all this."

His eyes lit with excitement. "Oh yeah? What is it?"

"In a few minutes our fathers are coming over." She licked her lips. "They're part genie, and if you make the right wish, they'll be able to use their gifts to help you. You'll have more natural ability."

Betty dropped tobacco into her pipe. "He needs to learn the hard way."

"We don't have time for the hard way," Cordelia snapped. "Sherman needs to be an expert in about five minutes if he's going to give Slug and that other guy—"

"Widdon," Sherman said.

"Widdon, a run for their money," Cordelia explained.

"No one's letting me wish my way into my magic," I said.

"That's different," Cordelia explained. "You've been procrastinating your power. Besides, you have an actual magical duel to do. Sherman just needs to look good for a little while, earn the witches' and wizards' respect."

Thanks for that, I thought. "Speaking of, I need to get working myself. I still have a lot to learn if I'm going to at least give Lacy a run for her money."

I left my grandmother and cousins as they fussed over Sherman. He seemed to pay no attention to what they were saying as he stared at Amelia in wonder.

Wouldn't it figure that Amelia was completely unfazed by him? I nearly chuckled at the development but instead decided to bite my tongue and work on my own magic.

I headed upstairs to grab my things and found Stevie and Mattie up there.

"Stevie, you're back," I said.

Stevie picked something off the floor and brought it to me. I gasped. It wasn't as bad as the fake eye, but in some ways it was worse.

"Slug's hairpin," I said. "How the devil did you manage to snatch that?"

The guinea pig didn't answer. Instead he nuzzled his nose against the back of my hand. I obliged him and gave the little guy a good scratch.

"Slug will rip me apart if she knows I have this."

"It ain't any different than Betty keeping that wand," Mattie said, stretching into a bow.

"I guess not, but that was Betty doing crazy Betty things. This is a guinea pig stealing a hairpin." I turned the simple bit of steel over. "I suppose I'll have to figure out a way to return it."

"Hmm, maybe it can help you," Mattie said. "You never know. It might come in handy."

I pushed the sharp end through the blazer I was wearing. "I'll ask Rufus about it. He might know a way to get it back to her without being ripped apart himself. Or maybe I can give it to Sherman. He lives in their camp."

I rose and grabbed my purse. "Either way, I need to check on the animals at Familiar Place. Make sure they're all right."

I headed from my room and out the door. Before I left, I noted that Sherman, being surrounded by so many women, looked slightly dazed and confused.

Part of me wondered if that was the normal look on his face. Something told me that was a possibility.

I strode down Bubbling Cauldron and was only a few stores from my own when I saw a group of Order witches harassing the owners of Castin' Iron, the riding skillet shop Theodora and Harry owned.

"We're confiscating all these skillets in the name of the Order," one witch snapped. "We'll need them for the skirmish against the werewolves."

"You can't take our entire supply," Theodora said. "We sell to folks from all over the world."

The Order witch snatched a skillet from Harry's hands. "We don't care. We need these, and we're going to take them."

The witch raised her hand, and a skillet rose and banged Harry on the head.

"Ah," he shouted, falling down.

"Harry," Theodora yelled. She rushed over to him, kneeling beside his hunched figure. Blood trickled from a gash in his head.

"Wait just a minute."

All heads turned to glare at me. Oh, crap. *Had I said that? Why would I butt my nose into someone else's business?*

Was I kidding myself? My entire goal in life was to butt my nose into other people's business. It was what I did best, it seemed.

"What do you want, Pepper Dunn?" the Order witch snapped.

I steeled myself. This was so stupid, completely ridiculous of me. Why in the world was I about to draw more attention to myself?

I guess because Harry and Theodora were good people. I wasn't about to watch as good people were hurt. Not while I was living and breathing, that was.

I pushed my way through the throng of Order witches until I stood face-to-face with the head witch.

"I want you to leave my friends alone. Isn't it enough that y'all have entered our town and demanded that unless I come with you, you'll put Magnolia Cove on lockdown until you starve us out? But now you have to start taking wares from my friends? No. That is quite enough. These people work hard at their business. Y'all leave them alone."

The witch sneered. Her lips pulled back, revealing yellow teeth. Ew. Didn't she brush them? Even if they were coffee stained, I was pretty sure there was a spell to fix that.

"And just what are you going to do about it?" she said.

That did it. Anger rose inside me. Magic unfurled within me, and I could feel ribbons of light unwinding.

As I glared at the witch, her eyes widened. I lifted my hand, and she rose into the air. Her feet dangled as she kicked and screamed.

"What I'm going to do about it is fight every one of y'all if you insist on hurting my friends."

Magic and instinct seemed to take over. I felt powerful, unstoppable, and for a moment I wondered if I could turn a rock into ice. I loved a good distraction as much as the next person, I recharged my focus, pinning it on the witch.

She gasped for air. "Will you leave my friends alone?"

The witch nodded. She scratched at her throat. I relaxed my hand, and she fell to the ground, landing on her rear end.

I fixed my stare on the rest of the Order. "If any of y'all even think of hurting my friends, you'll get much, much worse."

With that, the witches scurried away, including the instigator, though she made sure to spit on the ground in front of me.

"Classy." I clicked my tongue and remembered Harry. I rushed over to him. "Are you okay?"

Harry smiled weakly. "You didn't have to do that, Pepper."

I waved my hand over the gash, and it disappeared as the skin seamlessly wove itself together. The only sign there had been a cut was the thin line of blood that remained.

"Nonsense," I said. "Of course I had to do that. They were bullying you. I'm afraid this week is going to get worse before it gets better."

Theodora took my hand. "We're with you all the way. No matter what anyone says, we know what that old witch wants to do with you and we don't like it. It's wrong to take a witch's powers. If Lacy was any kind of decent, she wouldn't do it."

A gentle smile tugged at my lips. "Thank you, Theodora. But I don't want y'all to bring attention to yourselves because of me. Your safety isn't worth it. I was here and I stopped them, but they're dangerous. All of them."

Theodora nodded in understanding. She helped me hoist Harry to his feet. "We'll help however we can," she said. "We're old, and no one's going to push us around."

I considered what she was saying. "In that case." I leaned in. "I know someone you'll want to talk to."

After parting ways with Theodora and Harry, I walked the rest of the way to Familiar Place. The golden key fit snuggly in the lock. As the tumblers turned, I felt a wave of comfort and satisfaction. This store was as much my home as this town.

The door opened, and the animals awoke. The cats meowed, the puppies barked and the birds squawked.

I fed and watered them all and had just pulled the hairpin from my jacket and was inspecting it when the door opened.

"Pepper, I thought you weren't supposed to go anywhere by yourself."

I glanced up to see Rufus staring at me.

"What do you expect me to do, stay inside all day while this town succumbs to Lacy and her evil fiends?"

"No." He crossed his arms. "I expect you to practice your magic. I don't have to remind you how important this is."

"First off," I said, annoyed that he was trying to parent me, "I haven't seen the animals here in days. They can't sleep forever. I know that when I'm gone, they go into a sort of magical stasis, but I have to see them. Secondly"—I lifted the pin—"I'm fairly certain this is Slug Worley's hairpin."

Rufus's eyes widened. "How did you get that?"

"The guinea pig brought it to me as a gift."

He crossed to me and opened his palm. I dropped the pin into his hand. "I'd keep that guinea pig."

"I agree, but what do we do with it?"

Rufus pinched two fingers together and lifted the pin so he was staring at the shaft. "Have you ever played ghost with anyone?"

I shook my head. "I have no idea what you're talking about. Ghost?"

He smiled, clearly amused at my naivete. "Say Slug had something to do with Bee's death. This pin will allow us access to Slug's most vulnerable thoughts and feelings. We'll be able to get her into a state that is relatively sedated, and when she's there, we can appear to her as Bee."

Lightbulbs flared in my head. "And when she's calm enough, she won't know we're tricking her. If she killed Bee, then she might just confess to us."

Rufus snapped his fingers. "Exactly. But we can't do it without the pin. This is the key."

It sounded great, but I thought Rufus was forgetting something. "We also need a way to get into the camp, or to at least get Slug away from everyone else so that we can speak with her."

He rubbed his jaw. "What if...what if we could find a way to incapacitate the entire camp? Make it so that they won't know what happened."

My eyes flared. I grabbed his arm. "We put them to sleep. Like in *Sleeping Beauty.* In that story the entire castle is put out for one hundred years. Obviously we don't need that long, only an hour or two."

Rufus smiled. "If I had to guess, your grandmother would know a spell that could do the trick."

I thought about Harry and Theodora. "And if I had to guess, we could find volunteers willing and able to help."

Rufus dropped the pin into my open palm and closed my fingers over it. "Then what are we doing here? We've got an enchantment to plan."

EIGHTEEN

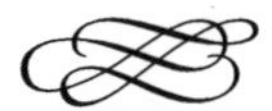

Turned out Theodora and Harry were happy to help us figure out a plan for putting the entire Order camp to sleep.

Before you ask, I did manage to carve out time to work on my magic but only managed to turn a rock into a flower.

Not anywhere close to ice. It was disappointing, but Hermit reminded me that I had to keep working at it. Hardly anything came easily, especially when it came to shifting elements. Or one form of matter into another.

But that had been earlier. Now the sun was burning down the horizon.

Betty stirred the cauldron over the everlasting fire. "The potion is almost done." She knocked the ladle against the pot and set it on a hook. "What's the plan?"

Rufus, dressed in black from head to foot, stepped forward. "The plan is someone's going to have to release the potion at the base of the camp. If we do this correctly, the fumes should overtake everyone in the Order and anyone outside. Whoever releases the potion will also fall asleep," Rufus added. "There's no way around that."

"What about Slug?" I said.

Sherman crossed his arms. "Leave that to me. I'll bring her back here."

"Where I'll rouse her with the antidote," Betty said.

"That's where you and I come in," Rufus said. "I'll use the pin to keep her in a state that's not quite awake. You'll do the Bee glamour, and we'll see what happens."

"What if it doesn't work?"

"Then we'll have a real problem on our hands," Rufus said. "It has to work or else there's no telling what Slug will remember or even do to us."

No pressure. I nodded and smiled brightly, suggesting I was ready for whatever would come.

"Cordelia, Amelia, Theodora and Harry will disperse the spell," Betty said.

"I'll go out and rouse them when we return Slug," Rufus said.

"I'll have the potion ready by then." Betty grabbed a handful of dried herbs that hung over the mantle. She crushed them in her hand and dropped them into the cauldron. Then, quick as lightning, she capped the cauldron and took a large step back.

"It's almost ready," she said. "I've got one more ingredient to add. Cordelia, get me the glass bottles and we'll ladle it up, add the last ingredient and cork the bottles before any of the potion can escape."

Within minutes everything was ready. Two hours after darkness fell, Betty nodded to the four who were to go.

"It's time."

Cordelia, Amelia, Theodora and Harry left. Sherman, Rufus, Betty and I remained. The seconds ticked by slowly as we waited another hour before we figured the potion had done its work.

Betty nodded to Sherman. "You're on."

Rufus rose. "I'll go with him. To make sure he doesn't have any problems."

"Are you sure?" Betty grimaced. "The potion should have done its work, but if you're caught, there won't be any saving you."

Rufus's gaze flickered to me. "This is much too important for anything to go wrong. I'll come if you'll have me," he said to Sherman.

Sherman extended his hand. "I'd be proud to have you." Then Sherman turned toward the door and tripped over the rug lying in front of it. A sliver of power shot from his hand, hitting a stalk of herbs fixed to the fireplace and setting them on fire.

Betty cringed. "Well, you're getting better."

Sherman wiped a hand down his face. "I'm working on it."

I smiled warmly at Rufus. I was glad he was going with Sherman. For goodness' sake, how had this kid managed to survive this long without killing himself or someone else?

Not a question I necessarily wanted an answer to. Once Sherman and Rufus left, Betty slumped into her chair. "We have some time before they return."

"How long?"

"Maybe fifteen minutes. Hard to say. More than likely Rufus will use magic to get them close to the camp. Then they need to make sure the potion worked, which it would have. Lastly Sherman has to find Slug and leave."

I folded my legs and sat on the edge of a chair. "I'm nervous, Betty. We've never done anything like this before. Did you tell Garrick?"

She nodded. "He wanted to come over, but I told him it would look suspicious. I figured he needed to know what was going on in his town, though."

I agreed with that. "We have to keep people safe."

Betty raised her hands. "How can we when the Order is so unstable? They're full of havoc." She eyed me. "How's the training going?"

"It's going."

"That's one thing you're not going to get out of—this fight with Lacy. Unless she dies first."

I clicked my tongue. "Know any murder spells?"

Betty shot me a scathing glance. "No, and even if I did, I wouldn't tell you."

"Figures." I tapped my fingers on the couch, trying to come up with a topic, any topic that would pass the time. "Seems Sherman likes Amelia."

"Almost as much as Rufus likes you."

I gave her a pointed glance. "We're not talking about me."

"I hope you're smart enough to realize who you're supposed to be with."

I nodded. "I am. I don't feel the same for Rufus that I do for Axel. We have chemistry, but it's different. I only wish he could find someone. Then maybe Axel wouldn't be so leery of him."

"I've got news for you, gal. Axel would be leery of him no matter what."

I rolled my eyes. "Thanks for that. Not that it helps."

"Rufus will find his own love one day. He doesn't need you."

"I agree."

"Don't forget that."

This was turning into a serious *come to Jesus* moment. "I don't need convincing."

"Remember, Axel and your love for him is the key to truly unlocking your power."

I studied her. There was definitely something suspicious going on. "How do you know that?"

"It's the secret of all true head witch power."

"Loving Axel is?" I said sarcastically.

"No." She scoffed. "I have heard that once your love is unlocked, a head witch can truly experience what their power is capable of."

"The closest I've come to unleashing true power, Axel was in my thoughts," I admitted.

"Good." She rocked back and forth, back and forth, seeming to contemplate something. "Just don't let Rufus get in the way of your thoughts."

"He doesn't," I snapped.

"Are you sure about that?"

I scratched my scalp, transmitting my frustration with this conversation into that action instead of saying something hurtful.

"Yes. No. There have been times when I haven't exactly been confused but I've felt Rufus's pull. There have been other times when I've been drawn to him but I know Axel is the one for me. Do I feel something for Rufus? Maybe, but it isn't a feeling that can go anywhere, simply because I don't see a future with him. I have a future with Axel, a real future. He has asked me to marry him."

She leaned forward, all interested and stuff. "And what've you said?"

"I told him I'd give him an answer when he returns. I actually want to go ahead and tell him, but he wants me to wait."

"Ah, maybe he's getting a ring."

I frowned. "How do you know there isn't a ring?"

"Because I don't see one. Simple as that. If you'd had a ring presented to you, some big flashy diamond, it would've been easier to cough out a 'yes' to Axel."

I glared at her. "I resent that. You're suggesting I'm only in it for the jewelry."

She shrugged. "All I'm saying is a diamond makes a decision easier sometimes. Not all the time but sometimes."

I shook my head. "You are something else."

Betty grinned mischievously. "Ain't I, though?"

A quiet overtook the room; the only sound was the crackling and hissing of the fire.

"I hope they're okay," I murmured.

Just then the door flew open and Sherman and Rufus entered, carrying Slug.

"Hurry," Sherman said, "get him by the fire."

I jumped up. "Who?"

"Rufus."

I reached for Rufus, who was ghostly pale. Sherman settled Slug down, and Rufus slumped into me. His eyes rolled back.

Betty rushed over to us. "What happened?"

"One of the guards showed up. He'd been out of Magnolia Cove on a mission and had arrived back after the potion was released. He caught us trying to get Slug. He hit Rufus with magic and I was able to stop him, but not before this happened."

"What about the guard?" I asked.

"I knocked him out and managed to work a forgetful spell on him," Sherman said. "But Rufus..."

Rufus was in a chair beside the fire. Sweat sprinkled his face, and his eyes were closed.

Sherman pulled back Rufus's cloak, revealing a wound beside his shoulder. Blood ran down his torso.

I shot Betty a worried look. "That looks bad."

"It was done by magic, you say?" she said to Sherman.

"Yes, magical wound."

"Pepper, get some cool towels. Your job will be to keep fever from setting in."

"Done." I rushed into the kitchen, grabbed a bucket and filled it with ice water. I dunked a few rags into it and hurried back to the living room. "I've got them."

"Get Rufus on the couch. The other witch will have to wait. I'll keep her sedated until we can get to her, but we need to help Rufus."

Sherman grabbed Rufus's head, and I grabbed his feet. Betty worked at the fire. She filled her cauldron with dried herbs and called up a rack full of magical potions and ingredients.

"Since I don't know what sort of spell caused the wound, I can only do a basic curing potion."

She worked while I placed a cold compress on Rufus's head. "He's getting hot."

"I'll work faster," she said.

Sherman stood by, his hands twitching in anticipation. "What should I do?"

"Make sure Slug doesn't wake up. I can only deal with one crisis at a time."

After a few minutes of Betty stirring, grinding and cussing, she brought over a thick paste.

"Cut his shirt off," she instructed me.

"Let me get the scissors."

I started to rise, but Betty pushed me back down. "With your magic. Do it with magic."

I nibbled my bottom lip, uncertain as heck as to how I was going to do this, but I couldn't let anyone down. I peeled back Rufus's coat and stared at the gaping wound.

I closed my eyes and imagined my finger cutting simply through the fibers of his shirt, not slicing any farther.

I opened my eyes and slid my finger from his shoulder to his belly button.

The fabric fell away. I peeled the clothing back and stared at Rufus's creamy skin.

Betty chanted something as she slathered the concoction of what smelled like roses and lavender over his skin.

"That should dress it," she said after a few minutes. She studied his form and her work. "His breathing is even. That's good, but we won't know anything for sure until he awakens."

"How long will that be?"

"Hopefully before sunrise. If he's not awake within an hour, we'll have to return Slug. We can't risk being caught in all this, even if it means our plans went wrong."

I nodded. Part of me wanted to question Slug, but most of me wanted to make sure Rufus was okay first. He'd done so much for us, for my family and me, I hated to think of him in anguish, hurt and suffering because of a plan we'd had.

I took his hand and sat beside him.

Betty pointed to Sherman. "You hungry?"

He patted his stomach. "I could eat."

"Come with me to the kitchen. I'll make us some food, and we'll discuss what happens if we have to get Slug out of here."

Sherman smiled. "Tell you what. You explain to me what to do, and I'll make the food."

A light glimmered in Betty's eyes. "I'll do better than that. I'll inform you on how to worm your way into Amelia's heart."

Sherman's face illuminated. Well, he was sold.

They left the room, and I stared down at Rufus. I squeezed his hand.

"Pepper?" he whispered.

"I'm here."

Rufus blinked his eyes open. "I can't see."

"What? Did the spell make you blind?" Oh no. That would be

horrible.

He blinked again. "False alarm. It just took a moment for my eyes to focus."

I nearly swatted him. "How do you feel?"

"Like I've been dragged through the streets." He smiled wanly and peered down toward his wound. "Should I look?"

I shook my head. "Not for a while. Betty slathered some stuff on it."

Rufus shook his head. "I don't know what happened. Out of all the sleeping witches there was one waiting for us, as if he knew what was going to happen."

I shook my head. "Impossible. No one knew but us and Sherman." My gaze drifted toward the kitchen. "Do you think?"

Rufus shook his head slightly. "I wouldn't believe so, but stranger things have happened."

"I hope he hasn't betrayed us."

"We need to talk to Slug." Rufus started to push himself up.

I placed my palms on his chest, stopping him. "Wait. At least a few minutes. She's still asleep."

Rufus gazed down at my hands, and I suddenly felt my face burning. I snatched my hands away.

"Too late," Rufus said smugly. "I've already felt your touch. You can't take that back."

"You're hallucinating," I said.

His dark eyes bored a hole straight through me. "You should marry Axel. You will marry him. You need to." He closed his eyes. "And I shouldn't be saying any of this."

I pulled a handful of hair over my shoulder and started braiding it. "No, you shouldn't."

"You and I can never be," he said, "not because you're with Axel, but because it's my penance."

"What do you mean?"

His eyelids fluttered, and Rufus glanced into the distance. "Because in my whole life you're the only person I've ever wanted to change for."

I sucked air. The revelation hit me squarely in the gut. "What?"

Rufus reached out. With the back of his fingers, he stroked at the loose hair around my face. "I wanted to be better because of you. Not for myself. It was foolish of me. For that, I don't deserve you."

I pressed the back of my hand to his forehead. "You're feverish."

Rufus grabbed my wrist. "No, I'm not, and if I am, I can at least blame this moment on that."

Rufus pulled me toward him, and I started to sink, felt myself tipping forward.

It felt like I was in a dream, that some otherworldly force was pulling me to him.

And it was wrong.

I jerked back at the same time the front door slammed open. My cousin Carmen Craple stood in the frame.

I rose. "Carmen, what are you doing here?"

She strode over, her red hair sailing behind her and her long legs striding quickly. "Betty called. Said you might need help pulling off a glamour with one of those horrendous witches from the Order."

I glanced down at Rufus. "Do you think you can do this?"

Rufus's mouth tucked into a thin line. Then he slowly nodded as mischief sparked in his eyes. "I'm already feeling better. Put on your glamour, Pepper. We need to know the truth."

NINETEEN

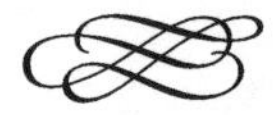

"Why have you called me here, Slug?"

I stood in front of the semiconscious witch wearing a glamour that made me look exactly like Bee.

Carmen held the hairpin after Rufus directed her on what to do. He was still too weak to manipulate it himself.

Slug stared at me with confusion in her eyes. "I haven't called you here. I didn't do that. I haven't."

I took a menacing step forward, keeping a firm scowl etched onto my face. "You want my seat in the Order. You're plotting to keep my son from having it. Admit it, you hate me. You've always hated me."

I raised my hands, watching as I shot rays of light around the room. Slug shrieked with fear. "Admit it, you killed me. You did it. You burned me to a crisp so that you could take my seat and so that Lacy wouldn't have anyone to fight against. Isn't that true?"

I slammed my fist into my hand. "Apologize to me now, or you will pay in the afterlife!"

I didn't know if that was true, but it sure as heck sounded great.

Slug recoiled. Fear splashed across her face. "Forgive me, Bee. Please forgive me, I was coerced."

Hope bubbled in my chest. "So you did kill me?"

She shook her head. "No, it wasn't me. Another witch came to me in my dreams, told me I had to place a fire stone in the bushes. Told me to put it there."

I shot Rufus a confused look. He made a slashing gesture across his throat, and Slug froze.

He tipped his head. "A fire stone is a magical stone that helps someone wield fire. If Slug had been told to place it in a particular spot, someone was obviously trying to make it look like she committed the murder instead of them. They may have used the fire stone to kill Bee, but if anyone saw the stone being placed, they would've watched Slug do it—not the real killer."

I frowned. "You're saying someone would be framing Slug."

"Right, and more than likely if Slug was interrogated about this, she wouldn't remember anything in the light of day. But here, since she's in between waking and sleep, she can recall the event."

"Ask her point-blank who did it," Carmen said.

Rufus snapped his fingers, and Slug returned to life. "Who told you to plant the fire stone?"

Slug opened her mouth, but no words came out. "Who was it?"

She shook her head. "It was—"

The witch started convulsing, choking on an unseen object. I shot a worried look to Rufus. He raised a hand, and Slug stopped.

He nodded to me to ask again.

"Slug, who sent you the dream? Who told you to plant the fire stone?"

She opened her mouth again. This time a ray of black sludge shot from her mouth and splashed against the wall.

"Ah," I screamed.

Carmen shrieked as well. Slug rose and seized. Her head snapped back, her shoulders hunched forward and she collapsed to the floor.

I flew to her, picking the witch up and staring into her blank eyes.

"There won't be a pulse," Rufus said, stepping over her body to get a better look.

"She's dead?"

He nodded. "She is."

Carmen's expression sank. "You were so close."

I closed my eyes and sighed. "Why? What happened?"

Betty's voice drifted from the back of the room. "Someone put a gag spell on her."

I twisted my head and shoulders to face her. "A what?"

"A gag spell," she repeated.

"That's so if she ever tried to reveal a person's identity, she would immediately die," Rufus explained.

I closed my eyes and sank onto my rear end. Slug's head rolled from my hands and hit the floor with a thud.

"So we killed her," I said.

"No." Rufus's hand gripped my shoulder. "Whoever gagged her killed her and Bee. They didn't want anyone to know who they were, so they covered their tracks."

"We're dealing with someone incredibly smart." Betty waddled over to the hearth and stoked the fire. "Perhaps the most powerful opponent you've ever faced."

"But what do we do now?" I said. "How do we find the killer and stop all this madness?"

Rufus picked up the hairpin and pressed his finger against the sharp end. A slow smile curled on his lips. "I think the best thing to do would be to send someone into the camp in disguise. Pretend to be Slug."

Betty cackled. "Great idea. Who's going to do it?"

"I will," Carmen said. "I despise the Order and want them gone."

I shook my head and rose. "No, Carmen. This isn't your fight. Lacy came for me and only me. If anyone's going to take Slug's place, I'll be the one who does it. I won't have anyone else trying to save me."

Carmen's expression twisted with worry. "Are you sure?"

I opened my palm to Rufus. "Give me the hairpin. I'll become Slug and invade their camp. We do this now."

TWENTY

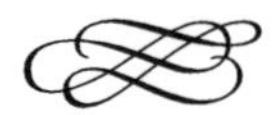

"You don't have to do this."

Rufus strode beside me, his long legs looking ready to sprint past me.

I shot him a sidelong glance. "Of course I do. This is my fight. *Mine.* If I'm going to figure out a way to truly defeat Lacy and get the Order to leave, then this is it. I can do this," I said more confidently than I felt.

I was a jumble of nerves, no doubt about that, but I wasn't about to let Rufus see. I'd made this decision, and I would stick to it no matter what.

"It's not that I don't think you can do it," he said. "It's that these people are dangerous."

"Gee, you think I don't know that, already?"

He placed a hand on my shoulder. "Would you stop?"

I exhaled loudly and turned to face him. The cool night air lifted the hair on the back of my neck, and the smell of grass trickled up my nose. It smelled like home—comforting and good.

It was the only good thing about the camp I was about to join.

I jutted my chin out and glared at Rufus. "What is it?"

"You don't have to do this."

Our eyes locked, and before I could do something stupid like crumple into a ball and start crying, I looked away. "Yes, I do. Once the Order discovers Slug is dead, Lacy will probably go ahead and challenge me. She won't wait, and I won't be ready. I'll lose."

Anguish filled his gaze. "I can help you."

I smiled. "You already have. You've given me so much. You've helped this town so much."

He looked away, scoffing.

"You *have.*" I took his arm and turned him to face me. "You must believe that. I believe that. You've been a great…friend."

His expression hardened. "As your friend," he said sarcastically, "I'm telling you this is dangerous."

"And as your friend, I'm explaining that I'm ready. Sherman is going to take me to Slug's tent so that I can be ready when the sleeping potion wears off. He'll show me what I need to know, and I'll spend the rest of my time figuring out who killed Bee and hopefully Axel will return soon with good news. If anyone can get a band of witches and a pack of werewolves together, it's him."

"Yes, he's a real miracle worker," Rufus said snidely.

"You can be too," I said.

We stared at each other for a moment. Rufus opened his mouth, and the words came out barely above a whisper. "You should call him before you go in. Let Axel know what's about to happen."

Sherman strode up from the dark. He turned to Rufus. "Are you ready? We have a lot of folks to collect."

Rufus nodded. "Our plan is to grab your cousins and magically transport them back to the house. We'll do the same thing with Theodora and Harry. That will give you time to acquaint yourself with whatever you need to."

"And search whatever I need to," I said quietly.

"Be careful," Rufus said. Without another word he pulled me into a hug. I hadn't expected it. Hadn't expected to feel his arms around me, to feel his muscles tighten and feel the rise and fall of his chest.

Least of all I hadn't expected to feel his heart beating against my throat. But it did.

I closed my eyes and listened until Rufus pulled away.

I knuckled a tear from my eyelid and followed the two men into camp.

Rufus helped me with my glamour, making sure the image stuck to me like glue and that it wouldn't dissolve even in my sleep. The last thing I needed to happen was to wake up looking like myself in enemy territory.

After saying goodbye to Sherman and Rufus, I strode into Slug's tent and sat. I pulled the phone from my pocket and dialed Axel. Since I didn't know when I'd be able to talk to him again, I wanted to at least let him know what I was doing in case something happened.

Or maybe it was best that I didn't tell him at all. Worry him less.

He answered on the first ring.

"I was about to call you." His husky voice pulled my heart and a lopsided smile tugged at my face. "How're things going there?"

What to tell him? The truth? It would only worry Axel. The best thing to do would be to skirt the issue.

"There have been some complications," I explained. "Nothing that you need to worry about, but a few things. How's it going there?"

"Well. I've got both sides sitting down tomorrow to talk over their beefs. I'm hoping to have this wrapped up quickly."

I clutched the phone and closed my eyes. "It's so good to hear your voice. I miss you so much."

"I miss you, babe." He cleared his throat. "Has Rufus been behaving himself?"

My lids popped open. "Yes. Why?"

"Just making sure. I don't want him trying to steal my lady while I'm gone."

"Rufus could never steal me. I'm yours. Always have been, even before I knew you."

Axel chuckled. "And I'm yours. I'll call you when I'm on my way back, okay?"

I sighed. "Okay. Be safe. I love you."

"Love you more."

I scoffed. "As if."

We hung up, and I slid the phone into the witch robes I wore. I took a minute to look around at the contents of Slug's tent. There was a cot, a trunk that presumably held clothing and whatever else she would've needed, a couple of tables and some chairs.

I pushed up my sleeves and headed for the trunk. "No time like the present."

The trunk didn't reveal anything of interest. Figuring I had less than an hour before the spell would wear off, I poked around the tents until I found the one Sherman had described as Lacy's.

It was made of black canvas and covered in silver drawings of moons and suns. It sat squarely in the center of the other tents and was a foreboding presence.

I swallowed a knot in the back of my throat. Yes, the structure intimidated me almost as much as the witch it belonged to. But I wouldn't have another chance to search it, so this was it.

I lifted the flap and nearly tripped over Lacy's unconscious body. She lay sprawled on the floor, a line of drool running from her mouth.

My heart ticked up at the sight of her, but I had to remember, I wasn't me. I was Slug, and Slug was friends with Lacy.

I shivered.

That thought made my dinner crawl up the back of my throat. How could anyone be friends with Lacy?

The room was similarly furnished to Slugs with one exception—Hugo sat in the back of the tent, chained to a post. My heart cracked in half at the sight of him.

He was asleep. The spell had worked on him same as it had everyone else. I crossed to my dragon and placed a hand on his head. His eyelids fluttered, but he didn't waken.

"I'll get you out of this, little guy. Don't you worry."

I inspected him. Hugo didn't look to have lost any weight, and there were no signs of abuse. Satisfied that he was being taken care of, if chained, I returned to my sweep of Lacy's room.

A trunk similar to Slug's sat in the center of the room. I tiptoed over to it and tugged on the lid.

Locked.

Of course. Lacy wouldn't leave her trunk unlocked. Where could the key be?

I closed my eyes and gritted my teeth. It would be on Lacy, of course.

I crossed to her limp body and proceeded to run my fingers along her pockets, searching for metal. I felt like a burglar, a really inappropriate one at that as I patted her down.

No key.

My mind raced. Slug's trunk hadn't been locked. I'd simply opened it. Placed my hand on it and the lid easily lifted. Or was I wrong? Had the trunk actually been locked the whole time but I'd been able to unlock it with the touch of my hand—or a hand that resembled Slug's enough that the trunk unlocked?

My stomach twisted. That was the answer. I knew it.

The trunk had recognized Slug down to her touch, and that's what had allowed me to open it. If I was going to delve inside Lacy's, I would need her to unlock it for me.

Or at least her hand.

The trunk lay in the center of the room, and Lacy lay by the front flap.

One of them would have to move, but which one?

A minute later I was praying the sleeping spell was still working when I hiked my arms under Lacy's limp frame and tugged her toward the chest.

She mumbled softly. "Don't make me drink that milkshake, all those extra calories."

I shook my head and continued to heave and yank.

Deadweight, even living deadweight, was heavier than I'd anticipated. But I continued on, finally reaching the rectangular trunk.

I exhaled and settled Lacy down. I grabbed her wrist and laid her hand on top. Hoping that was enough, I snaked my fingers underneath the lid and pushed.

It opened.

A squeal almost escaped my lips. I glanced down at Lacy. Her chest moved steadily, and her lids were firmly shut. I peered into the trunk and started madly searching for a fire stone.

Rufus had described it to me in detail. It would look like a chunk of silvery flint, with sharp edges. The rock would almost appear molten, and the weight would be surprisingly heavy.

I riffled through clothes and books, candlesticks and glass orbs, but I didn't find a rock. I searched again, just to make sure I hadn't missed anything, pulling the clothing and other objects out to pile them on the ground. I was careful, making sure I remembered how each piece had been placed inside. I didn't want to give Lacy a reason to think someone had been searching through her things.

But even on a second search, I came up with nothing. No fire stone. I went about putting everything back. I'd just closed the lid when a low growl filled the tent.

I glanced up to see Hugo awake. The dragon glared at me. Smoke curled from his nostrils.

My gaze darted to Lacy. Her shut eyes and even breathing revealed the spell still held her fast.

"Hugo," I whispered, "it's me, Pepper."

His growl deepened. It wouldn't work. He would think I was Slug. My voice sounded like hers.

But what about my scent? Surely that wouldn't have changed. I should still smell like Pepper.

I shot a furtive glance to Lacy.

Still sleeping.

I swallowed down a worry knot that was stuck in the back of my throat and crossed to the dragon.

His lips parted, and he bared teeth. I would not be frightened of my own familiar. I extended my hand for him to sniff.

Saliva dripped from his jowls.

"Hugo, it's me."

I placed my hand as close to his mouth as I dared. Hugo stared at me and slowly craned his neck to sniff.

"Come on, boy," I coaxed. "It's me. Mama."

Hugo inhaled deeply. His gaze flashed up to me, and I smiled widely. "See? It's me."

My dragon pulled back his lips, revealing more teeth. A second later his jaw opened.

I ducked as a stream of fire flamed from his mouth.

Panic filled me. Hugo screeched, his warning obvious. Get out or I would be scorched.

I left Lacy on the rug beside her trunk and headed into the darkness.

I knew I smelled like myself. Hugo would've recognized my scent. This could mean only one thing—Lacy had turned my own dragon against me.

TWENTY-ONE

"Do you think that sheriff is doing anything to discover Bee's killer?" I said to Lacy over breakfast the next day.

Luckily none of the witches had figured out they'd been subject to a sleeping potion. I had wondered if Sherman's forgetful spell would work on the guard who'd caught him and Rufus, but no alarms had been sounded after the sleeping spell wore off.

Lacy sneered at my question. "Do you think I care? Bee was a fly in the ointment. If she'd been able, she would have made sure we didn't come here. She needed to go."

Lacy peered at me. "I thought that's what you wanted, the opportunity for a seat?"

"I do," I added quickly, "but if someone killed her, why? And will they target one of us?"

Lacy waved away my concern. "I wouldn't think it mattered to you. It doesn't to me. For all we know, her own son killed her."

I laughed heartily at that, thinking it was a joke.

Lacy stared blankly at me. "Oh, you're not kidding."

She snorted. "Of course not. Everyone knows Sherman wanted Bee to teach him how to use his powers better. Being only half head witch, you would think he had more practice, more control. But he's a dimwit as well as a half witch."

Lacy threw back her head and laughed at her own joke. I paused but then realized that as Slug I would be laughing as well, so I did, being sure to lift my chin and chuckle as if her joke was the funniest thing I'd heard in my entire life.

Trust me, it wasn't.

Lacy leaned over and patted Hugo's head. My dragon was chained, which was good because every time he and I locked gazes, he growled.

Which was what he was doing now.

"I don't know what's gotten into him," Lacy said. "He didn't have a problem with you yesterday."

I shrugged. "He's an animal, Lacy, and a familiar to a silly witch, at that."

She stroked his head. "Yes, and it seems my plan to make him love me is working wonderfully. I only hope when he sees his old mistress again, he scorches her."

"I'm sure he will," I murmured, knowing that whatever Lacy had done to my dragon put him in her clutches.

"Tell me, what do you plan with the creature? I mean, once you've defeated Pepper, that is."

Lacy's eyes filled with lust. "Once I've shown the girl that she can't defeat me, with or without my wand, I'll take her powers, leaving her a shell of what she once was. Of course once that's done, I'll also find whoever stole my wand, kill them and then this little guy"—she smiled sweetly at Hugo—"will be turned into a new outfit with matching shoes and handbag, of course."

"Of course," I agreed.

My stomach squirmed, but over cups of hot tea, Lacy and I threw our heads back and laughed at our beautiful wickedness.

But what she'd said set my mind in motion. She hadn't killed Bee, but she thought that Sherman had.

I had my doubts about that. Sherman didn't seem like a killer. Unless he was the best actor in the world, that was.

I doubted he had that much talent.

But it also got me thinking that maybe there were clues inside Bee's tent, if it was still intact.

But how could I get in there without anyone thinking me suspicious?

After I left Lacy, I wandered through the Orders' ranks, trying to figure out a plan. It didn't occur to me until I was back in Slug's tent, staring at the ground.

From the corner of my eye I noticed something move. I glanced over and saw a little bit of white fur dart from one side of the tent to another.

"Stevie," I whispered. "Is that you?"

The small guinea pig scurried out from behind the trunk. His nose twitched as he sat back on his haunches and brushed a paw over his whiskers.

"It's me," he said. I wondered why he spoke sometimes and not others, but then decided it probably had something to do with the size of his brain—it being very small and all.

Was that prejudice, thinking that because his brain was small, his vocabulary was limited?

Probably.

"Did you follow me?"

The little guy didn't answer, but as he pawed his whiskers, something started protruding from his mouth.

"What is that?"

Stevie patted his mouth more and more until the thing came out.

"A wand," I said, surprised. "Bee's wand."

It was. Long silvery strands wound around the long piece of wood. "It's been missing," I said. "How'd you fit it in your mouth?"

"Big cheeks," he said.

No one had been able to find Bee's wand since the night of her murder.

Here it sat. Right in front of me and Stevie had found it. I traced my fingers over the silvery strands. The core wood felt charged, and the silver hummed as if ready to be used.

"Where did it come from?"

Stevie turned and started to dart from the tent. "Wait," I called. "Not now. We can't go out in the middle of the day."

The guinea pig turned and trotted back to me, stopping at my feet. He stared up at me curiously. I tapped the wand against my thigh, thinking.

"We'll go at nightfall. In the meantime"—I stowed the wand in my robe and picked up Stevie—"you need to stay out of sight. Think you can do that?"

Without missing a beat, the rodent scurried into my robes and hid. Now all I had to do was wait.

~

WHEN DARKNESS FELL, I released Stevie from my robes. The little guy had been a real trooper, staying quietly tucked away for the better part of the day.

But as soon as I felt it was safe to release him, I allowed the rodent to scurry on out into the camp.

He darted from the skirt of one tent to another. I followed, staying close. My gaze swept the area to make sure no one had caught sight of the little guy.

I grimaced just thinking what Lacy would do if she saw him. Poor little Stevie wouldn't last on the planet another second if Lacy had her way.

Finally the guinea pig dashed into a dark brown tent. It was a rich color and the material was suede. This was the thing about tents in the Order—no one knocked. If one witch wanted to visit another, she'd sweep the entrance flap aside and stride on in.

Needless to say, none of them had issues with modesty.

I opened the flap, but the tent was empty except for Stevie sitting in a chair.

"You found it here?"

The guinea pig hopped up and down to say yes. I frowned. Whose tent was this? I glanced around the room, wondering if I would another fire stone hiding somewhere.

There was no way I'd be able to get into the trunk. Even so, I moved to the center of the room where a trunk sat and placed a hand on it. When I lifted, it didn't budge. No surprise there.

I was standing in the middle of the room, still debating what to do when I heard someone enter.

"What are you doing in here? You can't be seen with me."

I turned around to find Sherman blocking my path.

My heart fluttered up into my throat. He'd had the wand. His mother's wand—one he could've only received if she'd died.

Perhaps that wasn't true. Maybe Bee had given him the wand before death.

But why wouldn't Sherman have said so? Why wouldn't he have simply admitted that he'd been hanging on to it?

It made no sense. No one knew what had happened to Bee's wand. Lacy had accused me of stealing it, but no one had found it. Until now.

Sherman had it.

I had to be honest with myself.

The only way Sherman Oaks could've gotten hold of Bee's wand was if he stole it from her.

I swallowed a knot in my throat and forced a smile. "I know, but I needed to speak to you." I made my voice louder. "You know you have no chance of winning against me. The voting will be soon, and as soon as it's done, we'll have that woman, Pepper. The Order will be able to leave, which is good because this town is running out of food."

Sherman eyed me suspiciously but moved to a chair and sat. He kicked off his boots and sighed. "It's been a long day," he said quietly. "All this magic practice is starting to wear on me."

I knew what he meant. I'd snuck off a few times to practice myself, but I felt like I kept butting up against a brick wall.

Something had to change or I'd never be able to beat Lacy.

I shoved that negative thought away. It wasn't something I needed to focus on. At least not right now.

"Sherman," I said tentatively, "I was wondering if you might have something in your trunk for a headache."

It was the stupidest request, but I knew he would fall for it. Sherman lifted one of his boots and turned it upside down. A rock the size of a marble fell from it.

"I got dragged face-first through the woods thanks to a spell gone wrong," he explained. Sherman turned his other boot upside down, and another stone dropped to the floor.

I smiled brightly. "At least you've been trying."

"Yeah," he said noncommittally. "Do you think if I improve my magic, it'll impress Amelia?"

I paused. I wanted to say, *of course it will, as long as you're not a murderer.*

But the truth was, though I hadn't spoken to my cousin about it, I had the feeling she resented the Order and everyone associated with it. If Sherman wanted to win her heart, he'd have to change his affiliation.

This was worse than warring college football team rivalries. Southerners were famous for loving their college teams. Once you picked one, you never switched. You were born into your affiliation at birth. I wasn't sure if the Order worked the same way.

"Um, I don't know, but I'll put in a good word for you. How does that sound?"

He grinned, looking very boyish. My heart lurched for him. He really seemed to adore Amelia, and let's face it, Sherman was kind of a buffoon—in a good way.

It was impossible for him to have killed his mother.

He rose and stretched his arms way over his head. "All right. Let me see about something for that headache."

He easily lifted the trunk's lid and started sorting through the pile of clothes and accessories. He pulled out a chess board, a toiletry bag, robes and finally found a small box. "This is powder for your headache. Mix one teaspoon with water. It should help. I could try to cure you with my magic, though, if you prefer."

I leaned back. "No thanks. I'm not interested in being dragged through camp."

He smiled sheepishly. "Can't say I blame you."

I took the box with thanks and peered into the trunk, spying something the color of lead sticking out from beneath a crimson-colored sweater.

I pointed to it shamelessly. "What's that?"

Sherman frowned. He picked up the clothes resting on it and set them on the floor. I knew what it was before Sherman had even plucked the object from the trunk and brought it into the light for me to see.

A round object with bumps and craters sat in Sherman's palm.

I frowned. "If I didn't know any better, I'd say that was a fire stone."

Sherman held my gaze. He studied me for a moment and then dropped the stone to the ground and ran.

TWENTY-TWO

I darted after Sherman, throwing open the tent flap and charging out.

The camp was dark and full of twists and turns. Tents dotted the path. Sherman had spent days there. He knew the way better than me.

I wanted to scream out, demand someone stop him, but I knew that was a mistake. What would Slug be doing charging after Sherman? How could I explain that we had been talking, that we had been in the same tent?

Everyone knew Slug hated Sherman.

I jumped over a cord and pushed myself on, pulling from the well of magic in my core. I felt the light unfurl, and my legs gained new strength, moving faster than humanly possible.

But not impossible for a witch.

Sherman reached the edge of the tents and was headed into a deeper part of the Cobweb Forest.

If he ended up in there, I might lose him. But on the other hand, this forest was my friend. The trees had shown me things before—the future, to be exact.

He headed in, and I dived after him.

The lights from the camp quickly disappeared under the dark

canopy. I opened my palm and wished I had made someone, anyone teach me a light spell.

Crap. I'd have to learn it on the fly.

I pictured an orb in my hand. My magic unwound, and next thing I knew, a ball of light danced in my palm.

I tossed it out. The light buzzed and flew, darting through the trees until it found Sherman and whipped around him.

Sherman swatted at the light. "Quit it!"

"Sherman, stop," I yelled.

"No! You'll never believe me!"

"Why'd you do it? Why'd you kill your mother?"

"That's what I mean," he yelled. "I didn't kill her!"

"Come back and explain it!"

"No!" He dashed off again.

But then he stopped and whipped around. Sherman raised his hand, and a dozen balls of light flitted above his head. The smirk on his face made my gut twist.

"Sherman?" I said suspiciously.

"It's time for me to stop lying. I did it. I killed my mother so I could take her place in the Order."

My lower lip trembled. "You've played us for fools."

"Of course I have," he sneered. "It was so easy. You want so much to be better than you are. Good luck. You'll never be able to stop Lacy, especially now."

Sherman raised a hand.

In that moment there were two things I knew. The first was that Sherman would shoot to kill. I had no doubt. One blast from him would end me.

The second was that I was fairly certain that as much as Sherman knew, he wasn't aware that some of the trees in the Cobweb Forest could move.

Lastly—I know I said two things but it was really three—I didn't want to kill Sherman. That was absolutely the very last thing I wanted.

I had no idea what alter ego had taken him over, but I raised my hand and shot first, smacking a tree in its center. The tree, not liking being hit, danced to the right, directly into Sherman, knocking him over and sending his magic firing straight into the night sky.

I shot again, this time much softer, and hit Sherman in the solar plexus. He reeled back, his arms pinwheeling. I raced after him and pulled the hairpin from my blouse.

I didn't need it to keep my glamour, which I was thankful for. I chanted a growth spell and looped it around Sherman's wrists, disabling him.

He kicked and whined. "Stop it! You can't win."

"Hold still," I yelled.

But Sherman was too strong. He broke the spell on the hairpin and rose. He whacked me in the head. Pain shot down my jaw, clouding my thoughts.

I couldn't think straight as stars filled my gaze.

Magic raged in Sherman's body, oozing out his pores in orange flames.

Y'all, I'm not kidding. Sherman looked like hell was about to unleash from his chest cavity.

He extended a large glowing hand at me. His lips pulled back into a nasty sneer.

"I did it. I killed my mother. She never wanted me to learn my magic the way she had. She said it was for my own protection, but she lied." He threw his head back and laughed. "And you—you thought you could win. You thought I would go down so easily. You were wrong!"

Power shot from his hand. I couldn't process. I couldn't move fast enough. I couldn't stop him. I would die here, in the middle of the Cobweb Forest.

What a crappy end.

I raised my hand just as a bolt of magic hit Sherman squarely in the chest, sending him spilling back into a tree. His head slammed into the trunk, and he groaned, slumping to the ground face-first.

My heart raced. I hadn't noticed its thunderous beat until now. My hands shook, and I forgot all about the pain radiating down my jaw as I looked around to see who had saved me.

I expected Rufus. I prayed it was Axel, even though I knew that was most definitely wrong. But I hoped and prayed that whoever had stopped Sherman was someone who was on my side.

A cloaked figure stepped out of the shadows.

I exhaled a huge plume of air. "Hermit?"

The iconic head witch extended his hand. "Are you all right?"

I nodded slowly. "He murdered Bee. I found evidence, and he ran. At first he said he didn't do it." I stared at Sherman's unconscious body. "But then he admitted it. Said he had killed her."

I dropped my head into my hands and wept. Hermit placed a hand on my shoulder. "Come now, Pepper. It'll be all right."

I stared blankly at him. "You know it's me?"

He nodded slowly. "Rufus asked me to keep an eye on you. Good thing I did. You almost got yourself killed."

I rose on wobbly legs and balanced myself on the strong hand Hermit offered.

"Come. Let's get you back to the camp before anyone notices you were gone."

"What about him?"

Hermit's mouth formed a thin, angry line. "I'll get him back. But now that it's been proven Lacy didn't kill Bee, expect her to come looking for you. Your time of avoiding her is done, Pepper. She'll be coming for you now."

TWENTY-THREE

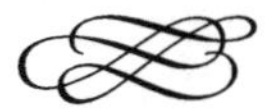

I returned to camp as Slug. There was no way around it. I couldn't disappear, and I couldn't simply throw off my clothes and reveal that Slug was dead and I had created a glamour to learn their secrets.

I mean, I couldn't, right?

Though it was tempting.

As Hermit carried a knocked-out Sherman over his shoulder, the moonlight illuminated his baby face. It seemed strange to me that he had spent so much time helping us. Sherman had even nabbed Slug and had seemed as surprised as we were about the gag spell.

Did Sherman even have the capabilities to create such a thing?

I got back to Slug's tent and readied for bed. Everyone would be tucked inside their tents as well, and it would be easy to escape, or to at least meet up with Rufus, let him know what had happened.

I texted him, and we planned to meet.

I made a big show of turning my lights off. Stevie had been waiting for me when I returned. He'd scurried up to me when I entered, and I scooped him up and buried my nose in his fur.

The guinea pig I barely knew was my only comfort.

He barely even talked, for goodness' sake. Turned out, Stevie didn't have to. He offered comfort even in silence.

After a little while I started out for the Potion Ponds, where I would meet Rufus.

I wove my way through the tents. A few muffled voices floated out from them, but for the most part silence filled the night. Grass crunched beneath my feet, and I cursed it, hoping the sound wouldn't betray me.

I had forgotten I wasn't Pepper Dunn, semi-talented witch with little training. I was Slug, a powerful witch who could probably snap a tree in two with her power if she wanted to.

Not that I'd seen her do it, but she certainly portrayed an attitude that she could.

As I exited the camp, I had the feeling someone was watching me. I stopped for a moment, turned around, letting my gaze wash over my surroundings.

No one was outside. A few canvas tents glowed with light. The wind rustled the trees and the leaves blew, but that was it. Nothing else could be seen or heard.

"My imagination," I murmured.

Shaking off the feeling, I made my way hastily toward my destination, slicing through the trees as a shortcut to the ponds.

But still the feeling that I was being watched lingered. I glanced over my shoulder several times but saw nothing. I had to push on, reminding myself that it was only my imagination.

I gritted my teeth, forcing away the eerie sensation, and crouched by the tree line.

Rufus would give a birdcall when he was in position.

The crystalline water reflected the moonlight beautifully. I sucked air as I realized the moon was full. I fisted my hands and cringed. Axel would be a werewolf tonight. So would all the others in the pack. They should keep each other safe.

I hoped.

I prayed that the peace he sought would be found. We needed proof of that peace if we were to get rid of the Order.

After a few minutes the call came. I slowly strode from the forest. If anyone had been following, they would see Slug walking to the ponds, alone.

I made a cutting gesture with my hand. Rufus would know to wait until I signaled it was okay for him to meet me.

After I stood staring into the pools for a few minutes, the creepy feeling that I was being watched vanished. I motioned for Rufus to come forward.

"You look terrible," he said, his voice full of worry.

I glared at him.

He laughed nervously. "I'm sorry. That came out wrong. But you look like you've had a time of it."

Rufus extended his hand. I studied his creamy skin for a moment before taking what he offered. Without thinking, I flung myself into his arms and let him hold me.

"Sherman killed Bee," I said through gulps of air.

"You must be wrong."

I shook my head. "No. I found the fire stone in his possession, and he admitted to the killing. He pretended to be our friend, Rufus. He was lying the entire time."

Rufus's jaw clenched. "Then he was an excellent liar." He sighed. "We trusted the wrong man."

"That's what I'm afraid of. He knows our secrets. The things we've done. If Lacy gets ahold of him and he starts blabbing, we'll all be in trouble."

Rufus gripped my shoulders and gently pushed me back. "We've heard from Axel."

Hope rose in my chest like a giant balloon. The pressure was so great I thought my rib cage would crack open.

"What did he say?"

"He's made progress. I believe they've reached an agreement."

The weight of his words released a boulder from my shoulders. "Thank goodness. We can be free of this mess."

Rufus's dark gaze bored into me. A shiver rippled down my spine. "Except for you."

I cringed. "I still have to face Lacy. I asked for it. I know it's coming. With Axel returning, we can reveal what happened to Slug, that Sherman killed her with the gag spell."

Rufus traced a finger under his bottom lip. "Do you believe that Sherman has the talent to work a gag spell?"

I considered the bumbling wizard I'd only recently met. He had two left feet and his magic seemed to be all tangled up.

Meaning he was pretty sad, y'all.

"No, but he admitted it, Rufus." I rubbed my temple. "That was strange, too. At first he said he hadn't done it and then something snapped in Sherman and he starting blabbing about how he'd done it. He tried to kill me, and then Hermit appeared and stopped him."

Rufus rubbed his chin. He stared into the pond, thinking. "I have a hard time believing that Sherman duped all of us."

I winced. "Me too. He seemed so genuine in how he bumbled around. It didn't feel like a role he was playing."

"Even the best of us are betrayed," Rufus said quietly. "Taken for a ride and cast aside at the end."

I cocked a brow. "Bitter much?"

He chuckled softly. "I'm not trying to be bitter. I only came because you contacted me, remember?"

"I wanted to tell you about Sherman and find out what this would mean—at least as far as the next few days are concerned."

"It means they'll try him for his crimes. I'm sure they'll do that first thing. If they have a confession, it will go quickly, but if they don't, it may last awhile."

"As in days?"

"No." Rufus shook his head. The breeze picked up, and his coat-tail lifted into the air. "As in hours. They'll torture him until he confesses, and even if he doesn't. He should though. It'll be better for him."

I gasped. "They're barbarians."

"They're witches, Pepper," he said sharply. "You've been lucky. All the witches you've known except for a solid few have been pillars of the community. Good people. This Order? This is what witches can become. Once you have power and talent, the world is yours for the taking."

"That's Lacy all over," I murmured.

He shoved a finger in my face. "And the rest of them, too. Don't for a second think they wouldn't do the same to you. Because they would, in a heartbeat."

I swallowed a knot in the back of my throat. "Okay," I whispered. "I know I'm lucky."

He nodded curtly. "Now. Thank you for explaining what you have, but I suggest you return to your tent and get a good night's sleep. There will be a trial, Sherman will be found guilty and then Pepper Dunn will have to face Lacy. There will be no other outcome."

"What if Axel returns?" I said hopefully.

"It won't get you out of it. You made a promise to Lacy. She will see it through."

Bitterness filled his tone. I frowned to the point I could feel wrinkles forming on my forehead. "I don't understand why you're angry so suddenly. Have I done something wrong?"

Rufus shook his head. "Of course you haven't done anything wrong. It isn't you—it's all of it."

I placed a hand on his arm. "All of what?"

Rufus snatched his arm away. "It's nothing." Anguish filled his gaze. "Do not concern yourself with me. I was once the enemy, remember? No better than this Order. In fact, if I could have been, I would've become one of them."

I shrank from him. "You've been bad, but you could never be them."

Rufus laughed bitterly. "Ah, Pepper Dunn, always the optimist. You think so? You've only seen in me what I would allow. You've never truly seen my heart."

"I have," I argued. "I've seen the good in it. I've seen what you can do. How you've helped people and how you've saved me."

Rufus shook his head. He pulled away and stared at the ponds. "I came because you asked. I've told you the news. You can be done with me now."

Then I realized what this was about. "It was because I told you I'm going to marry him, isn't it?"

He shook his head.

Exasperation filled my voice. "You said we should. You said Axel and I were meant to be. What do you think? I'm not any more confused? I have been. You've filled my head in a way I've never wanted or needed."

I fisted my hands. "So if you think that gives you a claim to being bitter, then so be it. But I refuse to be angry, especially at you."

"For so long," he said quietly, "I tried to convince myself that you were only a friend. That I wasn't really jealous of the wolf. Even when you tried to goad me the other night into revealing more, I wouldn't do it. I've placed too many barriers over my heart. But yes, I suppose the power of your words has finally hit me, made me realize that I've lost something before I ever had it."

He stared at me, his gaze drilling a football-sized hole in my chest. "And I don't know which is worse—losing something I've known, or losing something I never had to begin with. I think it's the latter."

I stepped back. "I don't know what took control of me that night. My magic—Hermit said I had to stop being confused about you."

Longing and sadness filled his eyes. I wanted to fling my arms around him.

"You know I've been just as confused about you as you were about me, I won't deny it, but—"

"But you and I would never work," Rufus said. "Once you fully knew everything that I've done, all the evil, you would hate me. Despise me. You'd see me as a monster." He hung his head. "And it's true. I have been a monster. I don't deserve redemption."

His voice dropped to a whisper. "The wolf deserves you. Not me. I don't say that so you'll feel sorry for me. I don't want your pity. That's the last thing I need."

Tears filled my eyes. All he required was my love, and I couldn't give it to him, not the way he wanted.

But I was through being confused about Rufus Mayes. I wouldn't survive my fight against Lacy if my heart was twisted with worry.

This needed to be put to bed, all of it. I didn't want to worry about Rufus. He was a man, one who had chosen his destiny and was on the right path.

I crossed the distance between us and put my arms around Rufus, squeezing him to me.

He hesitated, but then did wrap me in a hug. He smelled leathery, and I rested my forehead against his chest for a moment before breaking our embrace.

I slid my arms down his until I reached his fingers, where we both held on for a long moment before finally letting go.

I gulped down the few tears threatening to surface and said, "Goodbye, Rufus."

Before he had a chance to stop me, I slipped into the forest and disappeared from his sight.

TWENTY-FOUR

The next day I awoke to the sound of ringing bells. I heard others stirring in their tents.

I glanced down at Stevie. "Stay hidden." I pulled on a robe and marched outside.

The witches had all gathered in the center of the camp. Lacy stood beside Sherman, who was locked in a wooden yoke called a pillory, his hands dangling on either side of his head.

"What is this? The Middle Ages?" I murmured, referring to the antiquated means of punishment.

"I charge Sherman Oaks with the crime of the murder of his mother, Bee. He has confessed, my friends. So all we need to do is find a punishment that is sufficient. Then," she sneered, "we will take care of the Dunn woman and be gone from this place. Besides, I'm tired of this town, and food is becoming scarce."

My own stomach rumbled at the mention of food. I worried about my grandmother and cousins, wondering what exactly they had to eat. But if I knew Betty, there were probably jars of fruits and vegetables hidden away somewhere in the house. You never knew when you might have an emergency.

Even witches had to be prepared.

"Burn him," one witch yelled.

"Drown him," called another.

"Please," Sherman cried, "I'm innocent."

I frowned. He'd only confessed last night.

"You confessed," Lacy sneered. "You said you had committed this crime."

He clenched his fists. "I don't know what came over me. I don't know why I said that. It wasn't me. I wouldn't have killed her. Please, I don't have the talent to do such things like put a gag spell on Slug."

Every noise in the camp seemed to stop. No bird sang. No fly buzzed. The grass even stopped rustling in the wind.

Very slowly, almost as if in slow motion, Lacy turned to scan the crowd until her gaze settled on me.

"What did you say, Sherman?"

His face was red with emotion. I could almost make out tears spilling down his cheeks.

"Please," he begged, "I said I didn't have the magic to place a gag spell on Slug. The one that killed her."

He must've been delusional. He was tired. I couldn't blame him for spilling the truth. Sherman had endured a lot in the past few days—Betty helping him with his magic, his mother dying, her wand disappearing and reappearing in his room. His denial about his mother and then his admission.

To be honest, I felt as confused as Sherman.

Lacy stared at me. Fortunately my confusion wasn't enough to knock me from the present. I was quite aware that I wore the stolen face and clothing of a dead woman.

That would not be forgiven—not by Lacy.

"If Slug is dead"—her finger traced the sky until it landed on me—"then who is that?"

I tried to push down the panic, tried to forget that only about a year ago I had been a woman without the slightest trace of magic. I had been a loser, having lost everything in less than half a day.

I tried to push all that aside to remember who I was now—a witch with power, more power than even I had ever allowed myself to believe.

I threw off my own yoke, the glamour that shrouded me, and proclaimed for all to hear, "I am Pepper Dunn."

Lacy forgot all about Sherman. She screamed, launching herself at me.

I was ready for Lacy. Come what may, I would fight her.

An explosion rocked the camp. The ground rumbled. Witches were knocked over as it felt like an earthquake had parted the town in half.

"What was that?" someone shouted.

Lacy stopped, sniffed the air. She pivoted her body in the direction of the sound.

"My wand," she screeched. "It's my wand!"

Lacy forgot all about me and dashed from the camp toward the direction of the sound.

In that moment I realized what had happened. The wand must've gotten loose from its container and wreaked enough havoc at the Vault that it either blew off the front doors or blew off the roof.

Yes, the explosion had been that violent.

The rest of the Order ran with Lacy, forgetting all about Sherman.

Everyone but me, that was.

Why would Sherman deny, then admit and deny again?

I didn't like it, and I was going to get to the bottom of it. Without another thought I raced over and grabbed him.

Sherman's head lolled to one side. "We've got to get you out of here," I said.

"You can't," he replied. "They've got me."

"Not if I can help it, they don't."

I touched the pillory, but an electrical shock snaked up my arm. I winced. There would be no releasing him that way.

I hooked a hand under his arm. "Let's go. You've got to walk. Can you do it?"

"I don't know." He groaned. His pupils were large and dark. He wasn't completely present.

Crap. It would be up to me. I tugged Sherman, basically dragging him through the camp, running as fast as I could.

He stumbled, falling several times. I had to stop and pick him up, praying the entire time that we would make it. That the witches would be busy long enough for me to reach my house.

I was crazy. I knew I was, taking Sherman with me. But I couldn't watch him be murdered for a killing I wasn't convinced he had committed.

Finally, after what felt like hours, I reached Betty's cottage. Sherman's weight had taken its toll on me. My back killed me. My throat was dry. Sweat streamed down my spine.

The door flew open, and I turned Sherman to fit him through.

"What happened?" Betty said.

"He admitted to killing Bee, but I think he was coerced or spelled. I don't know which. But Sherman a killer?"

Betty tugged the black beret onto her head. "He's no killer, that's for sure."

Amelia and Cordelia took him from me and helped sit him on the couch.

"What were they going to do to him?" Amelia said.

"Burn or drown him."

She shuddered.

"What about the wand? What happened?"

"I did that." Rufus's voice caught me by surprise. He stood in the kitchen doorway, his gaze leveled on me.

I swallowed through my dry and scratchy throat. "Why?"

"Because I don't believe he did it, and I knew you would need a distraction."

Amelia groaned. "I'm dead meat."

Rufus's mouth quirked into a smile. "There's no proof you were the one who placed the wand there. None. Your secret's safe."

I pointed to Sherman. "We've got to get that thing off him."

Betty strode to the hearth fire and started grinding up ingredients and tossing them in her cauldron. "I'll get that solved. Give me a few minutes."

"They'll be here soon," I said. "Lacy will come. She'll know I'm gone, and she'll come for us. All of us."

I raked my fingers down my face. "I'm sorry. I didn't know where else to go. I've put y'all in more danger than I should have." I cringed. "I probably haven't even helped Sherman. All I've done is delay the inevitable."

"Pepper," Cordelia said, "we're here for you. No matter what."

"Yeah," Amelia added, "you haven't delayed anything. We will stand and fight with you."

I shook my head sadly. "There's nothing for you to stand and fight. This is my fight, *mine.*"

Amelia shook her head. "Oh no, we're sweet tea witches and we stick together."

"No matter what," Cordelia said. "Now, let's get this thing off Sherman and figure out what we can do to stop Lacy."

Betty turned away from the cauldron with a smug smile on her face. Mischief glinted in her eyes. "I think I've got just the plan. Sherman," she commanded.

Sherman lifted his lids and nodded. "Yes?"

"No matter what, you mustn't move. Even if you want to. Can you do that?"

He tried to nod, but it came out stiff. "I didn't kill my mother."

Betty ladled a green liquid into a cup. "I believe you." She crossed to him and brought it to his mouth. "Trust me and drink this."

Sherman took a few greedy gulps, grimacing at the taste. "What is it?"

Betty grinned. "It's a potion that will kill you."

LESS THAN AN HOUR later there was a banging at the front door. My cousin Carmen had heard about the commotion and had come over. "I'll get it," she said happily.

I braced myself, knowing what was about to come. My gaze

bounced from my cousins to my grandmother and finally to Rufus, who inhaled deeply, lifting his chest.

I did the same, remembering to stay strong.

Lacy barged through the door, her wand waving in the air. Magic spewed from it as if the thing was ready to serve justice to those of us who had locked it up.

"Where is he?" Lacy sneered. "Where's Sherman? You, Pepper, I'll deal with you later—and I *will* deal with you. But first I want the murderer. Where is he?"

Her words came out in yells and screeches. I pointed to the couch. "There. He's there."

Lacy whirled in his direction, took one look at the limp body of Sherman, which was growing paler by the second, and sneered. "What hoax is this?"

Betty took a menacing step forward. "No hoax. The boy killed his mother. He had admitted as much. My granddaughter was foolish to bring him here, so I did your justice. It wasn't by drowning or burning, but I killed him, one and the same. He is dead, and you have me to thank for it."

Lacy's jaw dropped. She quickly recovered and moved to inspect Sherman's body. "I don't believe you. It's a trick."

"No trick," Rufus said. "He's dead. Burn him yourself if you're unconvinced."

Amelia's gaze darted to Rufus. Lacy didn't notice. Instead the head witch placed a hand on Sherman and ran it over his body. After a moment she turned back to Betty.

"You've done the Order's work today. For that I'm grateful. It almost makes up for the fact that someone stole my wand, but not quite. There is still that to pay for."

Betty pulled out her pipe and lit it. She glared at Lacy. "I will unleash the guinea pigs."

Lacy shrank back. "The wand is forgotten about. But there is something else." She focused her attention on me. "You. We will meet today, in two hours. That's all the time you have left. All of it." She fisted her hand as if crushing something in her palm. "And then you will be ours."

"That is enough, Lacy. *Enough.*" Betty crossed her arms. "You can have the boy's body then. Since he died in my house, there are things I have to do—cleanses to make sure his spirit doesn't stay."

She nodded curtly. "Fine by me. He's a murderer anyway. Not only did he kill his mother, but I'm certain he's responsible for what happened to Slug. But"—she pointed a finger at me—"if I uncover you had anything to do with her death, you'll regret it."

"I would have a worse fate than you already plan for me?" I said snidely. "Impossible."

Lacy narrowed her eyes before whirling toward the door. "Two hours. The large park. You will be there."

As soon as the door shut behind her, I fell into a chair. I had two hours left. Let's hope they weren't my last on earth.

TWENTY-FIVE

We wanted to keep Sherman hidden, but Betty thought it would be best to take him out.

"Let them all see that he's dead," she said.

I shot her a hard look.

"Okay, so that they'll *think* he's dead. I'll wake him up tomorrow. Hopefully by then they'll be gone."

"One way or another," I mumbled sadly.

She patted me on the back. "You won't lose this."

I fisted my hands and prayed Betty was right, but I didn't know. Lacy wouldn't be a pushover, especially now that she had her wand.

I needed to be alone for a little while to gather my wits and my strength, so I went upstairs to my room.

Mattie greeted me with a yawn. "How're you holding up?"

I shook my head. "I hope I make it."

"You will." She jumped from the window seat and pressed her face to my leg. "I know you can do it. Just remember, if all else fails, throw everything you've got at her."

I smiled sadly. "Will do."

The next hour raced by, and before I knew it, I found myself standing at the park beside Bubbling Cauldron Road.

The place was packed. The entire town had apparently gotten word and had come to see me fight.

I hoped they'd come to watch me win and weren't betting on the opposite team.

"Keep your chin up," Rufus said. "Don't let them see your fear."

"I'm not afraid."

He shot me sidelong glance. "You are. But there's no reason to be. You'll defeat her. I know it."

I smiled at his faith in me. "Let's hope."

He glared at me. "You must not hope. You must know. Say it. Say you'll defeat her. And mean it."

I gritted my teeth and delved deep into my core. "I will defeat her."

He nodded. "Good. Don't forget it."

We walked to the front of the park where stadium-style benches had been erected. The stand was packed with witches and wizards.

"No pressure," I mumbled.

At one end of the benches Lacy stood with her Order friends. Hugo paced beside her. When the dragon saw me, he hissed.

I closed my eyes. "She even turned my dragon against me."

"It's a spell," Rufus said. "That's all it is."

I stopped and stared at him. "I can do this."

"Do not apologize for using your magic on Lacy. She will throw everything she has at you. Do the same to her. Do *worse.*"

Betty strolled up. Sherman was lying in a floating box.

"I think he's going to be angry at you when he wakes up," I said.

She glanced over her shoulder to make sure no one was listening. "We kept him alive. That's what's important."

I nodded. I didn't have anything else to say. All my energy had to be focused on going out there and winning at any cost.

I pulled my phone from my pocket and handed it to Betty. I wanted to call Axel so much it hurt, but I couldn't be distracted. Hearing his voice might make me crack. I might give up all of this and run in the opposite direction.

Right now I had to be strong.

"Witches and wizards, I want to thank y'all for coming." Lacy's voice boomed throughout the park. "You've come to witness the fall of one of your own. Pepper Dunn has evaded the Order for too long, and now it is time for her to join us. She must join the Head Witch Order. We need her. I will prove to Pepper that her selfish actions—not coming with us and forcing her own people to suffer because of it—have been stupid."

Lacy petted Hugo and smirked. She'd taken my dragon, sent my love away and had no conscience when it came to starving my people. *She* was the monster, not me. Lacy thought I should simply discard my free will because that was what she wanted. That was what was in her plan.

But that wasn't what was in my plan.

"Are you ready?" she said.

I nodded.

"Step to the ring."

A ring had been set up. A bald circle of earth, it looked forlorn and pathetic in the middle of the lush green park.

"We will begin as soon as we're inside," she announced. "We will be magically locked in. Neither of us will be able to leave until the other is defeated—by either giving up or death. Those are the rules. Are you ready?"

I glanced at my family, at their sad faces.

I would not hug them. I would not say goodbye because that wasn't what this was.

I stepped into the ring, and so did Lacy.

A *whoosh* of magic flared up on all sides, creating a barrier that enclosed us.

Lacy smiled wickedly. "No one can hear us. It's just you and me. Are you ready to bend to my will?"

"I will not bend to you. You've been the mastermind behind all of this. Did you kill Bee and then your friend Slug?"

Lacy shook her head. "I had nothing to do with that. Nothing. Time to meet your maker."

But I was ready for her. Lacy raised her hands. Fire spewed from her wand.

I pulled Bee's wand from my pocket. The wand with the silver wrapped around the wood. This was what Bee had been going to give me, I was certain of it. This wand wasn't just a wand that she used for spells; it was the opposite of the poison ivy wand.

It was ice.

A stream of ice flew from the end, hitting Lacy's magic squarely in the center and causing the fire to peter out.

"You would use Bee's wand?" she sneered.

"I would use whatever I can."

She gritted her teeth. "See if you can defeat this."

Her assault came harder and stronger. Lacy sent balls of fire, spears, arrows, anything she could at me.

But I was ready. From the tip of Bee's wand I shot the same back at her. We were evenly matched.

Lacy roared in anger as her assault did nothing.

Sweat poured from her face. It trickled down my back. She threw her wand to the side, growling in anger.

"Enough! I'll never win this way. No wands!"

She flicked her hand, and Bee's wand flew from my grasp, clattering against the ground.

Lacy flexed her fingers. "I will beat you. You will crumble, and if I have to do it the old-fashioned way, then so be it!"

She cupped her hands. A ball of flame grew in their midst.

Panic started to flutter in my chest, but I pushed it away.

I would not lose now.

Gasps from the crowd threatened to distract me, but I couldn't let that happen.

My gaze darted to the bald ground. There were no rocks, no stones, nothing that I could use to transform. Lacy's ball grew larger.

I glanced around hurriedly, trying to figure something out. Finally I picked up a clump of dirt and whirled on Lacy.

I didn't have time to duck as the fireball hit me squarely in the chest.

Agony does not describe the pain that flowed through my body. The crowd gasped as I crashed against the wall. The fire was gone, but every muscle in my body felt as if flames were wrapping around them and squeezing tight. Every inch flared in pain.

I gritted my teeth. I could not let her win.

"You thought you had me, didn't you?" She strode over, scowling. "You did not. I will break you, Pepper. In front of all your friends and family. It's too bad your boyfriend isn't here to witness it, too. It's a shame he won't be able to watch as I crack you in half."

She raised her hand again.

The time for doubt was gone. I curled my fingers into the dirt, grabbed a clump of the sandy stuff and flung it at Lacy.

All I wanted was to live.

The clump spread out, forming a wall of ice that hit Lacy squarely in the face.

She staggered back. That fueled me. I dragged myself from the ground and stared at Lacy as she wiped ice shards from her skin.

"You will pay for that," she screamed.

A great commotion in the stands grabbed my attention. Axel had arrived. Our gazes locked from across the park. My heart lurched at the look of anguish on his face.

He wanted to be in here with me, helping.

I could not let him down.

A great wave of fire flared before Lacy. It rose around her. Fingers of fire licked the sky as a tornado of flames engulfed her.

"You will bow to me," she screamed.

I clenched my fists, knowing what was coming. I looked inside myself, reaching for my power, reaching for the waves of light that I knew existed deep within me.

I searched for ice, tried to make it come, and it did. Snow and ice gushed from my hands.

Hope flared in my chest and then extinguished when Lacy's firestorm ate my wintery blast.

"You can't defeat me," she said. "I am a witch of the Order. You don't have the power."

Then I reached down, fighting for what I knew lay in the pit of me. I tugged and pulled as Lacy shot a blast of fire forward.

Come, light, I said silently.

Everything happened at once. The flames licked at me. Their heat nearly scorched my skin. An arrow of fire flew from her, aimed straight at me.

I closed my eyes and felt the magic, the power that lay dormant in me, unlock.

"End this," I said.

My power unfurled. A line of magic wrapped around Lacy's spear of fire, and like a hand closing around a rope, my power nabbed her fingers of flame and crushed them.

"Stop her," I commanded.

The power circled Lacy. Her face filled with fright.

"What are you doing?" she yelled.

"Ending this," I said. "Your reign of terror in the Order is finished. You will no longer harm others."

My power batted away Lacy's wall of flame as if it were nothing more than tissue paper. The fire died out, and my power wrapped itself around Lacy.

"You are finished, Lacy."

I cut my arm across my chest, and the magical wall that surrounded us vanished.

"What?" she said. "How?"

But the force within me was like a thousand years of witchcraft had unlocked. I could feel power all the way to my toes. It was a living, breathing thing, and Lacy's pathetic attempt to hold others, to hurt them, was nothing compared to the magic I wielded.

I turned to those in the Order. "The Order is finished here. This woman has been defeated. No longer will you follow her. No longer will you invade towns and hold them hostage."

Power coursed through me. It wasn't even as if I was speaking anymore. I had given myself over to my magic, allowing it to take control.

I glared at the witches on the stands. "And if any of you want to challenge me, please do. I am ready. I am willing, and I am able to take you on."

The witches stared at me. Their gazes locked on Lacy, who lay trapped under my magic. They stepped forward toward me.

I turned back to Lacy. "And to prove that this witch is no longer your leader"—I crossed to Lacy and placed a hand on her chest—"I will lock her magic so that she can never access it again."

"What? No!"

Lacy screamed and wiggled, but for all she had done to harm others, it was over. I pressed my hand to her chest and pushed. Every ounce of magic she had retracted, became impossibly locked in a spell that could only be broken by me.

The loss of her magic was too much. Lacy fell back, fainting.

I whirled on the rest of the Order. "Who's next?"

Then, as if I were dreaming, the witches that remained rose to their feet.

"All hail Pepper Dunn! She's freed us from Lacy."

I rocked back on my heels, shocked.

"All hail Pepper," shouted another.

Then, one by one, the witches who I thought hated me, who I considered evil to the core, fell to their knees in thanks.

In that moment the magic I had tapped into petered out as I stared at a wave of witches kneeling before me.

My gaze snagged on Axel. I reached for him, and he ran from my family. He crossed the distance within seconds. I fell into him as his strong arms wrapped around my waist. My energy drained away. It seeped from me, retreating to the recesses of my body, where it had started from.

"I love you," he whispered. "I was so worried."

I gazed into his blue eyes. "I love you. I can't hold on much longer."

He smiled gently. "It's okay. You can sleep."

My lids closed and I did.

TWENTY-SIX

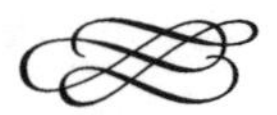

Axel's face was the first one I saw when I awoke. I threw my arms around him and held tight.

I didn't want to let go—ever.

"I'm here," he whispered. "I'm not going anywhere."

"Thank goodness," I said. "I missed you so much."

I lay on Betty's couch. Axel sat beside me. He threaded his fingers through mine and kissed the back of my hand. "I brokered a peace deal between the witches and werewolves in the South, so the Order wouldn't have had a leg to stand on."

I smiled weakly. Using my magic like that on Lacy had taken most of my strength.

"What happened again? After I locked Lacy's magic, I mean."

A luscious smile curved on his lips. "Turned out, they hated Lacy. All of them, and wanted her gone. But no one could overthrow her. Or no one wanted to."

I took Axel's hand and pressed it against my cheek. "I don't want to be their leader."

He smiled. "I think you're safe. I believe Hermit has taken that role now."

"And Sherman?"

Axel smirked. "You'll have to talk to Betty about Sherman. I think she's still working on waking him."

I sighed, and then another thought hit me. I bolted up. "Hugo!"

Axel patted my hand. "He's back to normal. I heard that Lacy had spelled him. He's okay."

As if on cue, Hugo bounded into the living room, placed two paws on the cushion, rose up and licked my face.

I laughed. "All right, I understand, boy. You're better."

The rest of my family entered. Betty and my cousins smiled and offered me congratulations.

"We were so worried, Pepper," Amelia said. "But we always knew you could beat Lacy."

"Yeah," Cordelia said. "None of us had any doubts."

"Your training suited you well," Rufus said.

My gaze flickered to him. I shot him a sad smile. "Thank you. But where is Lacy?"

"Whisked away by the Order," Betty said. "I believe her punishment is banishment."

"And Sherman?" I said.

"With Hermit," Amelia said. "He's trying to fix Betty's almost-death potion."

Betty sniffed. "It didn't need fixing. I almost had him awake."

I pushed myself up. "I want to see him."

Axel rose with me. "You need to go slowly."

I shot him a wide smile. "I'll go slowly if you take me to him."

Axel brushed a strand of hair from my cheek. His hand slid to the back of my neck, where it lingered. "I'll take you even if I have to carry you."

Love wrapped around my heart and gave it a good squeeze. "I'll go wherever you can carry me."

I walked slowly, but I managed to get into Axel's old Land Rover. Residents of Magnolia Cove filled the streets. The town had returned to life as the Order slipped away.

"Did I miss anything fun while I was gone?" Axel asked.

"I put on a glamour and went undercover," I murmured.

His jaw clenched. "Glad I didn't see that. I never would've let you do it."

"Then it was a good thing you weren't here. Axel, I—"

"Not yet." He glanced over. His stern gaze made my throat close. "Not here. You're not giving me an answer in my truck."

I clamped my lips. "Fair enough."

We arrived at the few tents left of the Order's camp. We got out of the car, and I shied away from the stares of the witches.

Axel's arm curled protectively around me. "They revere you. Few witches have that kind of power. Don't be afraid of them."

We reached the tent I knew to be Hermit's and stopped. I squeezed Axel's arm. "I would like to see Sherman alone. If that's okay."

He glared at the tent as if expecting it to reach out and snatch me away from him. "Let me look in first."

I knocked on a pole, and Hermit's voice filtered through. "Come in."

I lifted a flap and showed Axel that it was safe. He nodded warily. "I'll be out here. If you need anything, and I mean anything, get me."

I kissed his cheek, letting my lips rub against his stubble. I took a moment and breathed him in—leather and pine, pine and earth—and was thankful that he was home, that he was back with us, with his family.

I released my hold on Axel and found Hermit over Sherman's body. He didn't turn around when I entered, and I suspected he knew it was me by some unseen force of magic the Order wizard owned.

My footsteps took me just behind and to the side of Hermit. I watched quietly as he stared down at Sherman's body.

"It was a simple plan, really," he explained. "There would be a skirmish, we would go South and your power would take us there. Your gifts would fuel us, give us more magic than we'd ever had before."

He chuckled softly. "But you're too smart for all of that, aren't you? Too smart to be held and captured. Too smart to even let Lacy destroy you."

A cold chill washed up my spine. Hermit was talking to me. He stared at Sherman, but his words were clearly directed toward me.

"And now my Lacy is gone, banished to a magical island where I'll never see her again."

This was bad. I'd been in this situation enough times to know that Hermit was about to engage me. I couldn't do this alone. I was still weak from fighting Lacy. I needed Axel.

I glanced toward the tent flap.

"Don't even think of having him help you. Once you stepped into my tent, you were sealed from the outside. Sealed off. No one can hear you."

He laughed maniacally. "No one can help you." Hermit pivoted toward me, pulling the cowl back from his head. Malice glittered in his eyes. "You've destroyed everything I worked so hard to build."

My face twisted in confusion. "Everything you built?"

He gestured to the small tent. "I built the Order into what it was, but no one wanted to follow me, Hermit. I was too quiet, kept too much to myself. So I created Lacy."

He saw my look of surprise and nodded. "Created her, yes. Stole someone's power and fueled Lacy with it. She was hard and evil. Witches and wizards loved to hate her. They adored it. She was relentless—you knew that. You'd experienced it yourself. And she came here to attain our ultimate prize—you."

I clenched my fists as anger whipped through my body. "That's not a prize—a witch whose powers were to be stolen."

"No, and Bee was against it, of course. She didn't want to do that to you."

I shook my head sadly. "Which is why you killed her."

"She told me her plan. Even Bee didn't know my relationship with Lacy, didn't know who I really was, so she told me. I couldn't have her ruining my plans to attain your gifts. So yes, I killed her with something as easy as a fire stone. Her bumbling son could've even managed that."

Hermit chuckled. "I set Slug into action and planted the wand and the fire stone in Sherman's belongings to confuse the situation even more."

"But why did you care? If you owned the Order as you said, why would it matter that you killed Bee?"

Hermit paused. A look of humanity filled his face, and for a moment I understood—guilt. This was about the face Hermit showed the outside world and the true face he wore behind closed doors.

He pretended to be good, wanted to be loved. He'd needed Lacy to be the bad witch while he pulled the strings from the background all along, keeping himself looking pure.

He was a fraud.

"I couldn't be tarnished," Hermit explained. "They couldn't suspect me. Hermit is too gentle to do such a thing. Once you are in the Order, you follow whoever is your leader, and Lacy never did anything without justification. Coming here to you was justified. Dealing with the werewolves in the South would be justified as well."

He took a threatening step forward. "Even taking your power would have been justified. The Order called you to fight, and you ignored us, spitting in our faces. Rufus believed I was good, one of the few left, so he asked me to train you."

"And all the while you were setting me up for disaster," I murmured.

He shrugged. "You did manage to pull your magic together without my help."

I rubbed my forehead. "But your technique—to turn an inanimate object into something else—it's nearly impossible to do, isn't it?"

He cackled. "Nearly. But you managed. I wondered if you would," he said wistfully. "I thought—if anyone can do it, you can, Pepper Dunn."

His expression filled with wonder. "And you did. You turned dust into ice. You out-magicked my Lacy." He reached for my hair, and I ducked. "You are a worthy prize. Even though you've shattered everything I've built, I will still have you. You will join the Order and take Lacy's place."

He laughed. "See? I will still have my prize."

Hermit lunged for me. I jumped from his reach. "Playing hard to get, huh?" he sneered. "It won't help you."

He was right. I glanced left; I glanced right. There was nowhere to go, and I was tired. Adrenaline fueled me now, but how long would it last?

I raised my hand. A spiral of magic shot from me, wrapping around Hermit.

He threw back his head and cackled. "You may have beat Lacy, but you don't have the strength to take me on. I'm filled with the power of several witches. I can last for days."

He flexed his arms, breaking the magical bands as if they were made of tin foil.

He grabbed for me. I dodged again, throwing myself to the back of the tent. "You will surrender," he growled.

"Never," I yelled.

I threw another line of power at him. Hermit easily dodged it, hitting my magic with his hand and throwing it across the room.

The realization of what was going on sank in—he was incredibly powerful, and Hermit hadn't lied. Whatever witch's powers he had eaten or absorbed had made him nearly indestructible. I had beaten Lacy, but it hadn't been easy and I was tired. Fatigue had settled into my bones.

Hermit was fresh. He could fight for days while I only had minutes left inside me.

I dug deep, throwing everything I had left at him. My magic bounced off, dissolving in puddles on the floor.

"Enough of this." Hermit extended his hand, and a rope of power wound around me.

I struggled. I fought. I did everything I could, but his magic held me fast.

"You won't get away with this," I screeched. "I will fight you. I'll never give up."

Hermit smirked. "My dear, you've already lost." He cupped my chin. I jerked my head away, but he grabbed me fiercely, forcing me to glance directly at him. "Let me look in your eyes one more time, once more to know the anger burning inside you. In a moment that will all be gone and in its place will be submission."

He raised his hand. Power swirled in his palm. It was coming for me. I cringed. I didn't want to see what would happen next.

Then a loud *thunk* shattered the humming sound of magic. Hermit released me, and I heard something slump to the floor.

I blinked my eyes open. Standing where Hermit had been was Sherman, the giant pillory in his hands.

He dragged his gaze from the floor, where Hermit lay unconscious, and leveled it on me. Sherman smiled broadly. He tapped the wooden pillory.

"You know, I figured this would come in handy for something. I just didn't know what until now."

Hermit's hold on me vanished, and I threw my arms around Sherman. "You were right, Sherman. And when it came down to it, you knew exactly what to do."

"No two left feet for me," he said proudly.

I smiled. "Nope. Looks like your two left feet might be gone."

He nodded to Hermit. "Come on. Gather every witch you can. It's going to take all of Magnolia Cove to hold him."

I raced for the tent flap. Sherman didn't have to ask me twice.

TWENTY-SEVEN

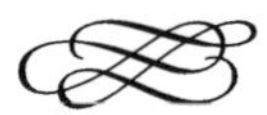

So the entire town of Magnolia Cove, along with what was left of the Order, got together and secured Hermit Mage. The wizard fought, but the combined powers of so many witches stopped him from breaking his bonds.

Garrick Young tipped his fedora at me. "We've already heard from the council. Those who worked with Hermit and Lacy have been kicked out, so the council is on our side once again. He'll be transported to them for his punishment."

I rubbed away a shiver that raced down my arms. "Thank goodness you're not going to keep him here, in the prison caverns."

Snaking underneath my town was a prison. I knew I would never sleep well at night knowing that Hermit was so close by.

Garrick scrubbed a hand down his cheek. "No, ma'am. This man's crimes are too severe. The council will deal with him. They may well seek to banish him like what was done to Lacy. Hard to say."

I thanked Garrick as he carted Hermit away. Most of the sheriff's department would escort Hermit themselves. Betty offered to go with them to keep the spell strong.

I hugged her and said my goodbyes. She clipped my chin with her knuckles. "You did good, kid. I'm sorry he fooled us."

"All of us," I said.

She nodded and joined Garrick and his men. Rufus stood off to the side. He had offered to help as well. I approached and gave him a big hug.

"Thank you for everything."

He scoffed. "I almost got you killed."

I shook my head. "You didn't know, Rufus—about Hermit. He hid his evil side well."

Rufus nodded curtly. "Make sure the wolf takes good care of you."

A weak smile wobbled on my lips. It was emotional saying goodbye to Rufus, but it had to be done. "I will."

Rufus nodded toward Axel and joined Garrick and the others. I noticed my cousin Carmen approached Rufus and watched them talk for a moment.

I wondered if something had sparked between them—something that hadn't been there before.

Sherman strode up to me. "Pepper Dunn, because of you I've become the new leader of the Head Witch Order."

My jaw dropped. "You're kidding."

He shook his head proudly. "Voted in unanimously—even by the witches who had already left. Thanks to you I've finally earned their respect."

"No, Sherman. Because of yourself you did. It had nothing to do with me."

He raked his fingers through his mop of curls. "Doesn't matter. Either way, I will bring the Order into a new day. No longer will we seek to prove we're better than others. Our mission now will to be to find other head witches and help them learn their powers. We will be a refuge for those who need us, a safe haven."

I couldn't help but grin from ear to ear. "Sherman, that's the best news I've heard all day."

He shot me a lopsided grin. I watched as his gaze drifted to the side. I twisted my head and noticed that his attention was pinpointed on Amelia.

I elbowed his ribs. "You might have a shot now. I think you should go find out."

Excitement flared in his eyes. "Thanks, Pepper. I can only hope."

After Sherman left, I drifted over to Axel, who had been watching me from the side, his arms crossed and a proud smile on his face.

When I reached him, Axel draped an arm over my shoulder. I laced my fingers through his, and we slowly walked from the camp, heading back to Betty's cottage.

We were silent for a few minutes until I finally broke it. "You know, I almost feel bad for Lacy. She was Hermit's puppet."

Axel stiffened. "She was only his puppet because she allowed herself to be. Don't feel badly for her."

I thrust my hip into his. "Why? Because it makes me soft?"

"You are anything but soft," he said huskily. "When I arrived, I saw you out in that circle and I wanted to yell and stop you. I could have. The peace treaty had been signed by the two sides. There was no reason for the Order to want you."

"It wouldn't have worked," I said.

He dipped his head toward mine. "It would have long enough for the wolf to come out."

I inhaled a deep breath of air and stopped, turning to him. I cupped Axel's beautiful face in mine.

"I don't need you to save me."

He threw back his head and laughed. "You've proven that. You don't need any saving. That's the last thing I want to do."

"Good," I said smartly, throwing my arms around his neck.

He dropped his hands to my hips and squeezed. "You got plans tonight?"

I smiled shyly. "I don't know. What do you have in mind?"

He stared up at the sky, an innocent expression splayed on his face. "Oh, I don't know. I thought maybe a little dinner, maybe some dancing?"

"Did a new club open up?"

Axel shook his head. "Nope, it sure didn't. But that won't stop me."

I giggled. "Sure. I'm free tonight."

"Great. I'll pick you up at six."

~

"HE'S GOING to ask you, you know that, right? This is it," Amelia squealed. "Now hold still while I get your hair put up."

I stood in the middle of my bedroom. Amelia curled my hair while Cordelia decided on my wardrobe.

"Uh, not black, it's too dark." She tossed a dress into the air where it vanished. "Not red, it's too trashy."

"Red isn't trashy," Amelia said. "I'm planning on wearing it on my first date with Sherman."

My eyes flared. "You're going out with him?"

She nodded slyly. "Yes, and if anyone gives me a hard time because he's a little aloof, I'll be mad."

Cordelia and I exchanged a glance. "Of course we're not going to make fun of you," she said. "Well, at least not this time."

"We like Sherman," I added. "He's nice."

Amelia's cheeks burned bright red. "Thank you. Now hold still, Pepper. I'm almost done."

"Silver sequins," Cordelia nearly shouted, "that's what you need."

Suddenly a silvery dress slipped onto my body. It flowed like silk and shimmered like diamonds.

"I love it," I said.

"All done." Amelia stepped back. "What do you think?"

I stared at the loose waves my crimson and honey hair were in. It looked gorgeous.

I pulled my cousins into an embrace. "Thank you. Both of you."

The doorbell rang. "He's here," Amelia squealed.

"Go get him," Cordelia said with more enthusiasm than she usually used.

I opened the front door and found Axel in a black suit and tie. His dark hair was swept back, away from his face. The ends just dusted his shoulders. His blue eyes blazed fiercely, and his clean-shaven jaw was set hard.

Axel was nervous.

"You look beautiful," he whispered.

"You look more handsome than a drink of water in the desert," I shot back.

He tipped his head and laughed. "You win."

I slinked my hand through his arm, and we headed out into the night.

We arrived at the Potion Ponds a few minutes later. A single table had been set up beside the sparkling water. Torches circled our dining area, and two plates sat covered atop the table.

I beamed. "Is all this for me?"

Axel kicked a stone. "No, I think it was for someone else, but they canceled at the last minute."

I punched his arm.

He laughed. "Yes, it's for you."

"Should we eat first?"

Axel shook his head. "No, I have a surprise."

Suddenly a four-string quartet appeared at the end of the pond. They broke into beautiful music.

Axel offered his hand. "May I?"

I slid my palm over his and nodded. "You may."

We danced slowly. The music flowed over us like water, and I stared up at him, total contentment in my heart. I smiled and he did the same, the corners of his eyes crinkling in happiness.

"Pepper, never in my life have I been as happy as I am with you."

I opened my mouth to agree, but Axel continued. "I want this feeling to last forever, and I want forever with you and only you, until the day I die."

Tear swelled in my eyes. Even if I had wanted to speak, all words evaporated from my mind.

I barely noticed when Axel stopped dancing. He pulled something from his pocket and dropped to one knee.

The lid of a black box snapped open, revealing a cushion-cut diamond flanked on either side by another smaller diamond.

"Pepper Dunn," Axel said in a low voice, "will you make me the happiest man alive and be my wife?"

My fingers trembled as I reached for him. I hadn't expected that—to be so full of emotion that my body would shake in this moment.

Axel took my hand, and I bowed my head, closing my eyes. When I opened them, my strength returned. I stared into Axel's perfect blue eyes.

"Yes," I said, "I will marry you."

Axel rose. He took the ring from the box and slid it over my finger. He smiled broadly. "A perfect fit."

I gazed up at him, and Axel dipped his head. Our lips met for a tender, romantic kiss. The music still played in the distance, soaring to a crescendo.

In that moment I realized Axel was right. I stared at him, and when I said my next words, I meant so much more than the ring; I meant Axel and our future life together.

"Yes, it is," I murmured. "It's perfect. All of it."

ALSO BY AMY BOYLES

SWEET TEA WITCH MYSTERIES

SOUTHERN MAGIC

SOUTHERN SPELLS

SOUTHERN MYTHS

SOUTHERN SORCERY

SOUTHERN CURSES

SOUTHERN KARMA

SOUTHERN MAGIC THANKSGIVING

SOUTHERN MAGIC CHRISTMAS

SOUTHERN POTIONS

SOUTHERN FORTUNES

SOUTHERN HAUNTINGS

SOUTHERN WANDS

SOUTHERN GHOST WRANGLER MYSTERIES

SOUL FOOD SPIRITS

HONEYSUCKLE HAUNTING

THE GHOST WHO ATE GRITS

BACKWOODS BANSHEE

BLESS YOUR WITCH SERIES

SCARED WITCHLESS

KISS MY WITCH

QUEEN WITCH

QUIT YOUR WITCHIN'

FOR WITCH'S SAKE

DON'T GIVE A WITCH

WITCH MY GRITS

FRIED GREEN WITCH

SOUTHERN WITCHING

Y'ALL WITCHES

HOLD YOUR WITCHES

SOUTHERN SINGLE MOM PARANORMAL MYSTERIES

The Witch's Handbook to Hunting Vampires

The Witch's Handbook to Catching Werewolves

The Witch's Handbook to Trapping Demons

ABOUT THE AUTHOR

Amy Boyles grew up reading Judy Blume and Christopher Pike. Somehow, the combination of coming of age books and teenage murder mysteries made her want to be a writer. After graduating college at DePauw University, she spent some time living in Chicago, Louisville, and New York before settling back in the South. Now, she spends her time chasing two preschoolers while trying to stir up trouble in Silver Springs, Alabama, the fictional town where Dylan Apel and her sisters are trying to master witchcraft, tame their crazy relatives, and juggle their love lives. She loves to hear from readers! You can email her at amy@amyboylesauthor.com.